Edward Lee's

HAUNTED

HOUSE

Overlook Connection
»» 2009 ««

HAUNTED HOUSE
all stories © 2007 by Edward Lee

Dust Jacket & Interior Illustrations
© 2007 by Glenn Chadbourne

"Haunted House," first published in this collection.
"The Room," first published in this collection.
"Night of the Vegetables," WHITE HOUSE HORRORS, edited by Ed Gorman
and Martin Greenberg, DAW Books, Sept., 1996.
"Secret Service," THE UFO FILES, DAW Books, Jan., 1998.
"The Hiccup," Camelot Books, a limited-edition chapbook, Summer, 2004.

This Edition Published 2009 by
Overlook Connection Press
PO Box 1934, Hiram, Georgia 30141
www.overlookconnection.com
overlookcn@aol.com

First Edition Trade Paperback
ISBN-10: 1-892950-89-8
ISBN-13: 978-1-892950-89-5

A signed limited hard cover of 500 copies
is available from OCP and Specialty Bookstores.
You can view complete details at:
www.OverlookConnection.com

Book Design & Typesetting:
David G. Barnett/Fat Cat Design

CONTENTS

GLENN CHADBOURNE

NIGHT
OF THE
VEGETABLES

He could see it in the tabloids. *Christ,* he thought. THE PRESIDENT CHECKS INTO WALTER REED ARMY MEDICAL CENTER... WITH CRABS!

"Crabs, Mr. President?" asked Dr. Greene. A real smug smartass, this one. A light colonel, Chief of Dermatology. Short, muscular, a fucking human fireplug. The pursed lips struggled not to smile. *Probably a goddamn Republican,* the President thought. *If he blabs, he'll be taking temperatures in fucking Alaska...*

It was so humiliating, but what else could he do? He'd told his assistant press secretary it was just a routine check-up. You couldn't keep anything from anyone these days. *The minute you become President, they pry into your life with a fucking proctoscope, the fuckers.* And—Christ!—if the First Lady ever found out...

"You're right, Mr. President," Greene agreed. What an image this must be: an army doctor on his knees, a magnifying glass in hand, while the Chief Executive of the most powerful country on earth stood before him with his pants down, having his crotch examined.

"Yes sir, they're crabs, all right. Or, technically, sebaceous pubic mites. Looks like you gotta whole metropolis of 'em down here, Mr. President."

Funny guy. We'll see how hard he laughs in Alaska. "It's not like I can walk into CVS and buy a can of CROTCH KILL. So how about spraying some heavy-duty crab-killer down there and let me be on my way? I gotta country to run."

"I'll need to take a species sample, Mr. President." Now Greene wielded tweezers. "There are over five hundred different types of sebaceous mites; in order to prescribe the most effective medication, I'll need to identify the genus."

Maybe I'll prescribe my foot to your ass, doctor. See if you can identify that. "Yeah, yeah, fine. Just hurry it up, huh? I have to propose a new tax bill to the Senate Finance Committee in about twenty minutes."

What a day—what a *year* for that matter. Ethnic cleansing in Macedonia, new revolutions in three more African countries, the goddamn Republicans threatening to filibuster again, and now this. *I got a smartass army doctor plucking at my dick hair with tweezers.* Could things get any worse?

Quick raps on the door, then a barking voice. "Mr. President. We just got a P4 priority call on the flyline."

It was Clegg, the Transport Team Captain, SS. The President's penis jiggled when he barked back, "I'm busy!"

A pause from beyond the door. "It's a P4 call, sir. Chief of Staff Ketchum's on the line. You better take it."

"Aw, for God's sake, hang on!" The President, seething, pulled his pants back up, leaving Greene poised with tweezers the goddamn Pentagon had probably purchased for five hundred bucks. *How can things get any worse? Just watch.* Ketchum wouldn't be calling unless it was a true emergency.

He bolted out into the hall, where his team of Secret Service stood waiting, sunglasses, earphones in their heads, SIG P226's under their jackets. Clegg stood stiff as a wood post, cradling the opened briefcase which contained the transport phone. Another suit stood in the background holding the odd, circular briefcase known as "the football," which housed a mobile transponder relay full of coded permissive-action links, the means by which the President could launch ICBMs. *Christ,* he thought, *I hope I don't have to use that thing today. I was looking forward to dinner at Peking Gourmet.*

The President touched the phone. "Is this thing secure?" he asked, irritated. "I mean, I don't want my conversation to be in *People* Magazine next week."

"It's a single-channel discriminator phone, Mr. President," Clegg replied, his voice stiff as his posture. "Fifteen different discrimination prefixes are processed through the White House commo computer. The codes are changed three times daily, after which they're transmitted through five revolving hopper frequencies. In other words, Mr. President, this is a secure line."

You're going to Alaska too, smartass, you and that fireplug doctor in there. "Ketchum, huh?"

"That's correct, Mr. President."

He pulled the phone out of its mount, then inadvertently scratched his pubis. "What is it?" he demanded of the phone. "I'm busy. I'm here at Walter Reed for a check-up."

"A check-up?" Chief of Staff Dallas Ketchum inquired over the line. "That's funny, I heard it was crabs."

GodDAMN!

But the Chief of Staff did not banter. "Forget about your crabs, Mr. President. We've got a *big* problem. P'Tang, North Korea? Remember that liquid-metal nuclear reactor they built a couple years ago?"

How could he forget? "Yeah. That new design, the one that the NRC said could never melt down?"

Chief of Staff Ketchum paused, cleared his throat. "Well, it melted down, about a week ago, our sources are telling us."

"Fuck! Shit! Piss!" bellowed the President of the United States. "And let me guess, you asshole! The wind is blowing all that radioactive shit over here, and everybody's gonna die of cancer!"

"Nothing like…that, Mr. President." Another pause, another clear of the throat. "Keep your fingers crossed. So far the outbreak seems to be limited to the west coast."

"Outbreak?" the President questioned. "Outbreak of what?"

«« — »»

Like…carrots, Robby thought.

Weird. He could devise no other simile. "I don't know what's wrong with my skin," Karen Ann said. "I've been trying to get a suntan."

Robby frowned at the wheel. *A suntan, huh? Suntans aren't orange.* Maybe she was on some weird medication; after all, he didn't know her that well yet. He turned down Martin Luther King Boulevard. *Her skin is the color of…carrots!* he kept exclaiming to himself. No wonder she wanted to go to the drive-in tonight. Karen Ann *hated* drive-ins—("Tacky," she'd told him when he'd first suggested it. "Low class.")—but now she was begging to go, and that made sense, didn't it? At Palmer's Drive-In, no one would be able to see her ridiculous orange skin.

This would be his third date with her, and the other guys at Taco Bell, where they'd met, assured him that three would be his lucky number. So far no genuine action, just a little grabbie-feelie, a little of the old Kissy Face. But, Christ, she was good-looking. A true blue California blonde—or, for the moment, true *orange*. Robby every so often steered in order to deliberately catch a pothole, to throw a side-glance at those big 36C's jiggling. Robby's right hand had had many a vigorous workout thinking about them. And tonight, with any luck—

I'll be seeing them, he ventured. But then the anticipation dwindled.

I just hope they're not orange, like the rest of her.

He knew she was self-conscious about it too. Karen Ann was a motormouth, always chattering away. But not tonight—she'd barely spoken at all, except to complain about the odd, orange tint to her skin.

"I just don't understand," she lamented, appraising her forearm. It was tan three days ago. Now it was orange.

Dusk bled into the sky ahead of them. "Wait a minute," Robby considered. Of course! "Did you use any of that funky suntan lotion?"

She squinted at him, orange-faced. "What—"

"You know, that Quick Tan stuff. You put it on your skin and it gives you a tan without having to be in the sun."

"Of course not!" she replied, her vanity assaulted. "I have a *real* tan."

Uh-huh. A real tan? You look like a goddamn carrot. But Robby let it rest; girls never liked to admit they used that sort of stuff, just like they never liked to admit they dyed their hair. That was it, though—he'd figured it out! *She probably put too much of that stuff on her skin, and it turned her orange.*

"So what are the movies tonight?" she asked, quickly changing the subject.

Robby rode over a pothole. Bingo! "Uh, *Three on a Meat-Hook, Barn of the Naked Dead,* and *Cemetery Tramps.*"

"Not *horror* movies!" Karen Ann griped. When she did, she crossed her arms beneath her bosom, which further accentuated the obvious attributes. "I *hate* horror movies, Robby!"

"Look, you're the one who wanted to go to the drive-in. Palmer's is the only drive-in in the county— the rest closed years ago." But now he was being cruel. "No biggie. We'll go someplace else. You want to go hang out at Hilltop? Or how about the multiplex?"

Sheer terror flooded her ocean-blue eyes. Hilltop Mall? Or a multiplex theater? No way she'd want to go there. *Not with that Quick Tan gunk turning her skin the color of carrots!* he surmised.

She faltered, stifled a pout. "Well, I guess horror movies are okay."

Yeah.

Robby parked the Mustang near the back corner; he remembered back when he was a kid—all of five years ago—they'd sneak in here in the trunk of Cage George's Hemi 'Cuda, with six-packs of Schlitz tall boys that he'd rip off from Dad. *Those were the days.* But this was a *new* day, wasn't it? And hot stuff sitting right next to him. Before the first flick, James Woods came on, warning America's youth about the evils of cocaine. It took a while—like maybe five minutes—to break the ice of Karen Ann's disconsolation. But in the dark she eventually reverted back to her old, luscious self.

Because, in the dark, you couldn't tell that her skin was the color of carrots...

They slid into a clinch. Just the shampoo-scent of her hair caused a familiar turgidity south of Robby's belt. And those big, buoyant, wonderful 36C's pressed against him when his lips met hers...

Robby flinched. His movements locked up.

Just one post-high-school kiss was all it took.

"Robby, what's wrong?"

But what could he say? The inside of her mouth tasted like—

Carrots...

«« — »»

"Mom!" Jeannie Straker cried out. "Horace isn't eating! I'm worried!" As though it were a careful prize, she held the rabbit up in both arms as she strode to the kitchen with this dire emergency. "I don't think he likes that new rabbit food you got at Giant."

"Rabbit food is all the same, dear," her mother said, loading dishes into the Kenmore. Dad was in the family room watching baseball; "Goddamn Yankees!" he shouted. "Get that garbageman off the mound! If goddamn Ripken hits another home run, I'm gonna fly to Camden Yards and shove the bat up his—"

"Phil!" Mrs. Straker berated. "That's enough!"

But Jeannie wilted—nobody cared about Horace.

"He hasn't eaten in a whole day, Mom! He doesn't like that food!" But then— *Wait a minute,* she thought. *Lettuce!* Horace loved to eat lettuce! "Mom, do we have any lettuce? Horace'll eat that."

"I'll get some, honey." Her mother smiled tolerantly and opened the fridge. At least Horace would have something to eat now. Her mother's face, however, lost its smile when she reclosed the fridge. "Oh, I'm sorry, Jeannie. There's no more lettuce in the crisper."

Tears welled in Jeannie's 12-year-old eyes.

"But we'll get some tomorrow, and a different brand of the dry food." Her mother patted her on the head. "Don't be upset. Horace'll be up to his big ears in food tomorrow."

"I bet goddamn Chizmar a case of beer on this game!" her father railed from the other room. "I'm gonna lose *again!* And goddamn Mussina—the Yankees oughta buy him! Then at least they'd have someone who can pitch! Christ Almighty, I could pitch better than Keyes with my goddamn *feet!*"

"Phil!" Mrs. Straker raged back. "Would you *please stop yelling* about *baseball!* You're upsetting Jeannie!"

"*God*damn Yankees..."

Jeannie moped off to her room, cradling Horace. *They don't care,* she thought. *Poor Horace...* She sat down on the bed with her lethargic pet, scratching his head, rubbing behind his ears. "Don't worry, Horace," the little girl avowed. "We'll get you lots of lettuce tomorrow."

She lay back atop the bed, suddenly tired, and without forethought, then, she drifted off to sleep.

Ever dutifully, Horace the white rabbit sat beside her, his pink nose twitching...

But when little Jeannie woke up, her screams nearly shattered her bedroom windows. What had happened? She'd taken a nap, and—

Her eyes bugged. She held up her hand, but there really wasn't much of a hand remaining, just bones. All the skin, it seemed, had been stripped off her little fingers!

And, worse, on the bed lay a patch of dampness, a stain, but it wasn't blood. Jeannie knew it *couldn't be* blood because blood was red, yet this odd stain was the thinnest shade of green, akin, of course, to the color of lettuce.

Horace looked up at his screaming master, nose still twitching, and his tiny white mouth similarly stained...

《《 — 》》

"You've gotta be fucking shitting me!" bellowed the President of the United States. A closed session, now, in the Oval Office. Chief of Staff Ketchum was there, as was Secretary Sallee from HUD, Nutman from the Nuclear Regulatory Commission, and NSC Field Deputy Hodge.

"The contagion seems to have cessated, Mr. President," Sallee began. "We've received no reports of infection east of the Rocky Mountains. That's good news."

"Good news!" wailed the President. "Everybody west of the Rockies has turned into a vegetable, and that's good news!"

"First of all, Mr. President," continued Sallee, "the infection is selective—not everyone is affected, maybe only ten percent of those in the exclusion perimeter. And they're not turning *into* vegetables, sir, they're merely acquiring certain genetic *traits* of, well, of vegetable matter."

"You guys are all a bunch of assholes!" the President yelled. "Shit, I oughta fire ya all! How am I gonna get re-elected if a bunch of west coast twerps have turned into vegetables while I was in office? Christ, California? That's a fuck-load of electoral votes! And how the hell did this happen, anyway?"

Nutman, the NRC Chairman, was possessed of a suspiciously British accent. The President didn't like Brits; they reminded him of all those limeys on the infomercials, selling miracle car wax and dripless paint brushes. "It seems, Mr. President," Nutman began, "that the P'Tang reactor suffered what we would call a Status 4 Meltdown, which is quite serious, like Chernobyl. Standard first-response protocol is to smother the core. Generally this is done by pouring in wet cement from helicopters. But the Koreans, evidently, had no wet cement on hand, so they dumped in dirt."

"Dirt?"

"Yes, Mr. President. Soil from a nearby field." Nutman paused to light a Marlboro. "Regrettably, though, said soil was taken from a collective *vegetable* field..."

Now Hodge, from the National Security Counsel, spoke up, adding the minutia of speculative detail. "What we think happened, Mr. President, is that some very obscure mode of genetic transfection occurred in the reactor core. Live-Vegetable Fallout is what our experts have dubbed it. Then a peculiar occluded weather front broke into a high-pressure center, quickly feeding the Live-Vegetable Fallout into a massive formation of altostratus cloud banks. The high-pressure center carried it all over here, whereupon the altostrati released a short but heavy amount of 'trough' precipitation."

"And that's why Secretary Sallee referred to this as good news, Mr. President," Chief of Staff Ketchum jumped in. "It means the worst is over. More than likely, the transmission of this new disease has stopped. So there's nothing to worry about."

Spittle flew off the President's lips when he eloquently shouted, "Get the fuck out of here, all of you no-dick busted humps! You're all fucking fired! Jesus Christ in a fucking hotdog stand! U.S. citizens are turning into fucking vegetables, and you assholes are telling me there's nothing to worry about!"

《《 — 》》

And so ensued what would, in the realms of modern history, come to be known as The P'Tang-Reactor Vegetable Epidemic. The National Guard was helpless, panic erupted in the streets. Maternity wards soon became dispossessed of familiar, squalling babies, replaced instead by roughly nine-pound satchels of queer, human-shaped vegetables. Street gangs looted grocery stores en mass, routing produce sections only. Emergency room floors were once slicked in blood; now, though, they were slicked in stewed tomatoes, creamed corn, and something suspiciously reminiscent of V-8.

Chaos ran rampant.

The government passed bill after bill: The Omnibus Plant Matter Survivor Package, Seedling Care Reform,

The 1996 Vegetable Security Act, and, of course, the famous Civil Vegetable Rights Bill.

And, eventually, and by the grace of God, things got back to normal.

The United States Census Bureau, via crucial calculations made by the National Institutes of Health in Bethesda, Maryland, would in time estimate that no fewer than 26.7 million people were infected with TIVS—Transfected Irradiated Vegetable Syndrome.

But at least, as Secretary Sallee had guaranteed, no new case of contagion ever spread past the Rocky Mountains...

《《 — 》》

And, unfortunately, Secretary Sallee was wrong. A barometric anomaly known as an "altostratus high-pressure funnel" bloomed from the heavens during the contagion period. And, unfortunately, several hundred thousand more became infected with the dreaded TIVS.

《《 — 》》

"You motherfucking hunka walking shit!" shouted the President into his Oval Office phone shortly thereafter. "You gotta be motherfucking *shitting* me!"

It was Dr. Greene on the other end of the line, Chief of Dermatology at Walter Reed Army Medical Center.

"I'm sorry to have to tell you this, Mr. President," Greene apologized.

"I'll dig your eyeball out and piss in your head!" the President bellowed at the grim news. "I'll pop your balls off and hang them in my limo like sponge dice!"

Greene went on to explain, "Those crabs we thought you had, Mr. President? Those sebaceous pubic mites? Well, we analyzed them, sir, and they aren't sebaceous pubic mites after all. They're aphids."

GLENN CHADBOURNE

SECRET SERVICE

"**V**ictor four, six, forty-six delta, romeo nine, nine, forty-nine tango, echo eight, seven, forty-seven sierra," the old man muttered.

He looked up, however briefly, and caught Karen's eye, one of his own eyes long since obscured by cataracts. He smiled shakily, deepening the furrows of age.

Garand took Karen's arm, then loudly bid to the old man, "Ms. Lavender will be back shortly, Mr. President. She still has some processing to finish."

"It was, uh, nice meeting you, Mr. President," Karen said.

The old man held his smile on Karen. "Yes, yes, nice meeting you too, young miss. We'll watch TV?"

"Sure, Mr. President, all the TV you want," and then Garand pulled her aside and took her back into the house.

Some President, Karen thought through a smirk.

To be more correct: a *former* President. It was difficult to believe that this broken, half-blind old man sitting in a lawn chair, one Rowland Wilcox Raymond, had served two terms as the Chief Executive of the United States of America. *What a ripoff,* Karen thought.

"You see what we mean?" Garand said.

"Alzheimer's and a half," Karen said. Former President Raymond had been diagnosed several years ago—she remembered hearing it on the news. He was ninety-two now, and in otherwise perfect health.

"He just seems so...I don't know. Like someone's grandfather."

Garand chuckled dryly. "Well, in that case, granddad has a big mouth."

"A big mouth?" Karen inquired. "What do you mean?"

Garand shrugged. "He used to be the President, for God's sake, privy to the most sensitive information in the world—and now he's got Alzheimer's. Talk about a classified nightmare. Anything he might say, right off the top of his head, could jeopardize our national security."

"Oh, come on," Karen scoffed. "He can't remember anything important, can he? He's ancient."

"Ancient?" Garand shook his head. "Those numbers he was reeling off? They were permissive-action suffixes. You know. ICBM launch codes."

≪≪ — ≫≫

Fuck, Karen Lavender thought. However profane, it was a pale thought, and a hopeless one. Almost ten years on Uniform Branch—night duty at the goddamn Oman Embassy on Massachusetts Avenue. The closest she'd ever gotten to the White House was seeing it on a post card. All right, so her performance ratings weren't that high, and the 2.5 at Maryland probably didn't help, but— *It's because I never slept with the right field supervisors,* she felt sure. *That's why I never got promo'd to White House duty. Sexist pigs. Their brains are in their jockeys.* The only reason she'd joined the Secret Service in the first place was to guard the President— the *real* President—a critical service, a job with prestige and honor. *And because I didn't fuck and suck every pantload in the upper office, I get ten years of night shifts for a bunch of Arabs.*

It was true, at least, that Karen did not agree to carnal activities with *every* "pantload" in the upper office, just the wrong ones. It was mostly oral sex— Karen, of course, on the performing end, and with every ejaculation into her mouth came a similar promise: Certainly she would be transferred to White House duty very soon. She could count on it. Don't worry, Karen. You're there any day now.

Yeah.

But, lo, for all those years, the only thing transferred was semen from some guy's piss-slit into her mouth. *All those years,* she thought ruefully. *Sucking the dicks that didn't matter.*

And now...this.

Well, at least she got out of Uniform Branch, and the 2000-acre ranch in Sacramento was nice. But when she'd asked for the Presidential Security Detail...this wasn't quite what she'd had in mind.

"I can fly anything God can make," the President said. "I should've put USAEUR on Defcon One. Fuck 'em. The ice-cream—*that's* the answer."

"Senile *and* crazy," she whispered to herself.

"What's that, missy?"

"Nothing, Mr. President. I was just saying that it was very *hazy* today."

"Ah, yes, you're right. It was the Texas Mafia. LBJ knew all about it. And I can tell you this. There were four shots total but two of them came from the Dal-Tex Building."

Karen wiped spittle off his chin, refilled his anti-spill cup with Kool-Aid. After two days, she'd stopped being appalled. What was the point?

"All you gotta do is stay with him until eight a.m.," Garand, the Case Agent In Charge, had instructed. "Feed him, change channels for him, like that. Since his diagnosis, his sleep schedule's changed, a typical con-traidication of Alzheimer's. He's awake all night long, likes to watch TV."

Great, Karen thought. *My illustrious career forges on...with reruns of Three's Company and Gilligan's Island.*

"But *don't* let him out of your sight. He's crafty, there were a couple of times when he got out of the house at night. We don't want the President getting off the property and winding up on Route 40. Can you imagine if someone picked him up? He'd be spouting off our MIRV targets, or telling someone that Brezhnev was actually murdered with Prussic acid contact poison administered by a U.S. Army field operative."

Karen's spirit felt like a stone dropped in a well. *Plunk..*

"Cheer up," Garand said. "At least he can go to the bathroom by himself. Well...usually. Oh, and you don't mind cooking, do you?"

This couldn't be worse—or could it?

Garand stroked his chin as if he had a goatee. "That's all cake, but...there's one more thing."

"Yeah?" Karen asked.

"See, he's on all kinds of medication—you know, for his Alzheimer's—and some of these meds are new.

Vascular dilators, mainly. They increase his blood supply to the brain...but they also increase his blood supply to—"

"Yeah?" she repeated.

"Well, you know. To *other* parts of the body. Sometimes he goes into fits, and we don't want that. He needs to be...taken care of."

Karen's jaw dropped at the words.

"Look, if you don't want the job, I understand," Garand augmented. "We'll send you back to the Oman embassy and get someone else." Another stroke to the invisible goatee. "But if you *do* want the job...I can guarantee you White House duty after he dies. I mean, come on. How much longer can he live?"

Garand had a point. And if she was interpreting him correctly, he was asking her to sexually service a ninety-two-year-old ex-president. *That old?* she asked herself. Vascular dilators be damned. She seriously doubted a man that age cold sport much of a hard-on. And the fits? She could hack it.

"All right," she dismally agreed. "I'll do it."

"Great!" Garand rejoiced. "I knew you weren't a quitter! Thank God we've finally got a gal with some gumption!"

Karen was surprised by the level of his approval. Had other women been offered this assignment, and turned it down once they were informed of the fine print?

"But you *do* guarantee me that I'll get White House duty when—"

"When the old fuck dies, yeah. Guaranteed one hundred percent." Garand grinned sheepishly. "But, uh, there is one more, uh, little thing, ya know?"

Karen smirked. "What's that?"

Garand shrugged. "Just three or four times a week. No big deal, right? I mean, it's not like you haven't done it before, right?"

Karen's eyes thinned. "And that would be?"

Garand unfastened his belt and lowered his trousers and boxers. "I come real fast. Promise."

Karen stared at Garand's face, then his crotch.

Then she got down on her knees. *At this point,* she considered, *what's one more dick in my mouth?*

«« — »»

She quickly learned, though, that it wasn't *one* more dick—it was two. Karen actually didn't mind blowing Garand—he was right, he was fast—but he wasn't kidding about those vascular dilators. She hadn't been on her new duty for more than a couple of hours before former President Raymond, sitting on the couch, extracted an erection from his pants.

"Missy? I'm ready."

At first she thought it was a joke; she thought it was fake. But when he pulled back the abundant foreskin, she knew it wasn't rubber.

No fucking way! she thought. *Get the fuck out of here!*

The President's genitals were immense. Testicles the size of Szechuan dumplings depended in the wizened scrotum above which throbbed a penile shaft that looked like a peeled, foot-long plantain. With veins.

Karen hoped her stockings wouldn't run when she knelt down. A swallow, a blink, then a deep breath, and her face moved forward. She thought about the most unsexual things when the President's member docked with her mouth; she thought about Hummel figurines, the Telebubbies, and the engine grease under her very first boyfriend's fingernails (he worked on cars, but didn't have much of a camshaft).

Up and down, up and down, her well-practiced lips glissaded over the ex-President's sexual organ. He made peculiar noises from his throat as she commenced. *I'd have better luck blowing a french bread!* she thought in complaint. His crabbed hands feebled at the back of her head, pushing down, stuffing the immensity of turgid meat past her tonsils and down her throat. Up and down, up and down, seemingly forever. Those vascular dilators, indeed, did the job, but—

Would you hurry up and come! her thoughts wailed.

"Ah-ah...*oogie!*" he mumbled, his old convalescent legs trembling. Then, after an easy half-hour of fastidious sucking, the biggest cock she'd ever had in her mouth vomited plumes of semen down her throat. Karen hitched; at first she thought it might shoot down her windpipe into her lungs. Her nostrils flared for air, and when she finally pried her mouth off the fat prong, a last dribble spilled onto her tongue.

It was easier to swallow than to spit.

The executive penis deflated to something that reminded her of a slack ground-chicken sausage. With veins.

"Booglidoo, Missy," he complimented. "That was better than Nancy."

Drool dangled from Karen's lips as she kneed backward, dizzy. She supposed it was a compliment.

"All right," he said. "Now I'm ready for dinner."

«« — »»

Garand had the audacity to give her a card file of the President's favorite dishes. "Did you enjoy your dinner, Mr. President?" Karen asked, taking up the empty plate.

"Oh, yes, I'd like dinner very much. I would like corned beef and cabbage, and potato rolls please. And the Green Giant brand lima beans. The fordhooks."

Which was what he'd just devoured in a considerable portion only moments ago. Karen sighed.

"TV, TV! Magnum!"

Not a professional notion but an honest one: she saw herself wringing his old neck. At least then her life would be interesting, not this busy-work executive nanny blow-job administrator bullshit. At least she only had to blow Garand; she didn't have to change channels for him, or fix his meals, or wipe his ass. *My life is a wasteland,* she thought. Porridge was more interesting. A ten-pound bag of fertilizer was more interesting than this inept tragedy that was her existence.

Shortly after dinner:

"I have to poo," President Raymond declared to her.

If I kill him...at least I'll go down in history, she thought. Instead, she walked him to the bathroom, dropped his pants, and sat him down. He defecated noisily, in blurts.

"Wipe," he ordered.

Mom, Dad, see how I'm carrying on with my career?" she thought. Grimacing, she slid the pad of toilet paper up his crack.

"Ooo," he commented.

Then got hard again.

It flipped up like a police nightstick.

With veins.

"Sit on Mr. Happy," he said.

How about if I cut Mr. Happy off? she thought. She could envision the fat stream of blood draining into the toilet, mingling with his Oval Office shit. She stayed the impulse, though, remembering Garand's promise...and hoisted her skirt, rubbed spit into her majora, and sat.

"Sit on Fido. Wuff-wuff!"

Fido about skewered her. She could've sworn she felt the fat glans butting against her abdominal wall. *Goddamn it, would you hurry up and come!* she thought in a painful fury. Big dicks were fine, but not on ninety-two-year-old Presidents. He defecated some more, during the action, ribbons of excrement falling loudly into the toilet water as she rode him.

Then—

"Oogily!" he exclaimed. "Foogily moogily!"

How can an old mummy like this come so much! she thought in rebellion. Her vaginal vault flooded. When she finally pulled off, there came a sound like a cork popping, then a snake of hot semen ran down the inside of her leg.

"Gar-hoogily. Fido *liked* that."

Yeah, I'll bet he did... "Go watch TV, you fuck-head!" she yelled, dragging his pants up, shoving him out the door. "I've got to clean up!"

"Magnum!" he celebrated. "Magnum's on FX channel!"

This guy comes in quarts, she thought, wadding up more toilet paper and running it up her leg. It took several wads. And when she plopped them all into the toilet and flushed, the toilet backed up.

«« — »»

Weeks went by, then months. Every Monday, Wednesday, and Friday, like federal clockwork, she sucked Garand's small penis and swallowed his ejaculant. But so many more times than that she was forced to service the ex-president's trout-belly-white tubesteak. Twice a day, sometimes three.

Thank God for those vascular dilators.

One night she'd done the dishes after dinner, and when she was returning from the kitchen, she found the President finnicking with the lock on the french doors.

Pain in the ass. "Just where do you think you're going, Mr. President?"

"I'm meeting North and that ghoul Casey at the Old Executive Office Building. I've got to tell them to shred everything." He blew spit bubbles as she guided him back to his chair. "Casey wants one of his ops to hit Woodward. George thinks we should, and frankly, you'd need a crow bar to get into Hayworth's pants. God knows I tried."

Her mind blankened as she sat back. These slips of senility weren't even funny anymore; by now she'd heard it all: senseless prattle laced with startling utterances. "No, no, it was *Bobby* who did it, I heard Hoover's tapes. She was pregnant. Peter Lawford watched the door." "The *Thresher* was sunk by a Soviet nuclear torpedo." "It was Teddy and Dodd— Remember? The waitress at La Brasserie?—we told them we'd pay the girl off if they abstained on the Companion Bill to H.R. 214." All this and disturbingly more. Undisclosed missile sites, top secret radio frequencies, a White House nuclear self-destruct device, Mach 7 aircraft, secret listening posts, electro-magnetic-pulse beams aimed at a row of townhouses in

Reston, Virginia, C.I.A. heroin routes into Burma, and Vince Foster was really executed in Crystal City. On and on.

She didn't even care anymore. The system seemed to work for everyone else, leaving her with the shaft. What, a pissant COLA raise every year and a 401K? That's what life was all about? *I'm a Secret Service Agent in good standing and they make me be a baby-sitter! I have to wear an apron. I do dishes and fuck and suck a brain-rotten president!*

Sometimes she could just lump it all. Forget about duty and service. Do something for herself for a change. At 35, she wasn't getting any younger. Her once-plump breasts were starting to sag. Her vagina looked like ground pork.

Fuck, she thought.

They were watching TV. "Ooo-yeah," some ludicrous pro wrestler yelled. "Step into a Slim Jim!"

"What's a Slim Jim?" the President asked.

"I don't know," she dismissed, waving a hand. "Beef jerky or something."

"Well jerk this beef, bitch."

Karen turned at the slight. The President had already dug his penis from his pants. The gargantuan thing throbbed upward, tapping him on the belly.

Why don't you just die? she thought, but that thought hardly conformed to reality. The reality, instead, involved something else.

She grabbed the warm erection as if grabbing a cucumber. She began to jerk it. She jerked hard. *Christ, am I pumping up a fucking tire!* Eventually, a pearl of pre-ejaculatory fluid formed at the tip of the glans. "Fido's ready for you to sit on him," he informed.

That's just fucking great, Mr. President, she thought. *I couldn't be more elated to know that Fido's ready...*

She sat on Fido nonetheless; the President blew mindless spit bubbles as she fucked his lap. She rode him hard, hoping to get it over with quick, but then he shivered.

"Drew-hoogily! Suck Fido now! Suck him!"

Karen supposed if she smothered him with a pillow, she might get away with it. She supposed that if she just jammed his mouth closed and pinched his nostrils shut, he would die and no pathologist would bother to make checks.

But Karen didn't quite have the guts for that.

She lifted her ass off his penis—another cork unpopping—then resolved to finish the task. She knelt between his ancient, knobby legs, and sucked. The flavor of herself on his dick tasted salty, bitter, sort of like bad fish, and as she sucked more vigorously, her nose detected the clear evidence that the 3-11 shift hadn't bothered to wash the President today.

Kill me, God, she begged. *Just kill me now.*

The President's orgasm shot repeatedly into the back of her throat in thin, hot threads. It reminded her of egg drop soup: thin as water, salty, with immoderate mucoid lumps.

"Glew-googily," he exclaimed. "There's one for the Gipper."

Karen's teeth clacked together. It was just easier to swallow.

«« — »»

The clock ticked on like her life: without event. This was it. Change channels, wipe his ass, cook his meals, and fuck him and suck him whenever the electorate crane rose. On the limited occasions, when she'd simply refused the latter, Garand's warning rang true. President Raymond had launched into a fit of maniacal inanity, spouting CIA crypts, the names of directors he hated, and choice samples such as "Fuck Congress, we'll take up the slack by selling TOW missiles to Iran," "So what about Mena Airport! Bill's in on it, and so was George!" and "I fucked the shit out of Jayne! That blond bitch was *unconscious* when I was done with her!" It was an Alzheimer's circus tirade.

Easier just to suck and fuck him.

But what of her *life?*

There must be more to life than this, she considered.

When she looked, the President was picking his nose with one hand and scratching his crotch with the other.

Yeah, to hell with this, she gave serious consideration. *Start over again. Do something for me.*

"Alexander Haig was Deep Throat," he babbled. "Rogers assured me we could hide all our ADMs and W-79s from SALT II and the Russians would never know."

"What's that, Mr. President?"

More spit bubbles. "I was just saying, I had sex with Faye Ray once. They invented AIDS at Fort Dietrick in 1976, said it would wipe out the ghettos in five years."

Jesus.

Occasionally she nodded off and caught snatches of plush dreams. Lying on a beach in Cancun. Traveling Europe. Making love and having babies.

"You know the protocol. I need the SAC commander to authenticate confirmation of hostile intent. I don't *care* if our air-space hasn't been violated yet. What, I'm supposed to wait? Give me the discriminators! I'm the President!"

Her eyes fluttered open. She moaned. Now he was fervently pressing buttons on the remote as Tom Selleck switched to Jay Leno, then Jerry Springer, then Beavis. "Goddamn Andropov! I'll bury him! Watch me! See if he doesn't die of a heart attack!"

Yes. A real life instead of this farce. A nice house, a two-car garage. A white picket fence and a dog in the yard. Hubby mowing the grass on lazy Saturdays while she baked cookies... She was nodding again, words rupturing the sweet dreams.

"—million dollar offer posted last year, but so far, no takers."

A million dollars would be nice too, to make the dream just perfect.

"—verifiable evidence. How do you *prove* something like that?"

A handsome husband who never cheated on her... Attractive well-mannered children who earned good grades and didn't get into trouble...

Yes, it would be so nice...

The dream morphed into the face of a stuffy game-show host and a gaudy background made to look like a TV news room. The dream was gone. She was awake again...

"From Ubatuba, Brazil to Roswell, New Mexico, the mystery may never end, even with countless thousands of eyewitness reports. What's really happening out there? And just *what* is the government trying to hide from the public?"

Great. Now it was this UFO claptrap. One hokey flop after the next. At least Magnum was good-looking, killer butt, gorgeous pecs. And those eyes!

But when she turned her head to check her charge...

"Oh my God, no!!"

The President was gone.

I can't believe it! I fell asleep! How could I be so stupid!

She dashed to the kitchen, then the den, then the south hall. Nothing, and they were all locked accesses. If he'd wandered down to the foyer, the recept team would've seen him right away. Just as she would hit the elopement alarm—

snick-snick-snick

An odd sound to her left. Toward the bedroom. *Maybe the President's finally decided to take a shit on his own.* From the TV, more words droned on: "Fantasy-Prone Syndrome, systematized hallucinosis, shared delusional ideas of reference, and, of course, the primal human instinct to *believe* that we are not alone in the universe. The same can be said of every religion to ever exist. It's a functional mythology..."

Karen winced as a heel snapped off her shoe when she turned toward the bedroom, then a sudden pinching cramp reminded her that her period was starting and it felt like a gusher. This was not her day. But then she heard the sound again, another *snick-snick-snick.* followed by an even stranger wet, crackly peeling noise.

She limped into the bedroom, stopped, and frowned. "What are you *doing!*"

"The TV. Didn't you hear?" He was on his knees, his tongue licking the corner of his mouth as he dug at the floor with a pocket knife. He was peeling a tile off the floor!

"Mr. President, would you *please* give me a fucking break?"

He didn't hear her, removing the rest of the split tile. "Now I remember! LeMay gave it to me when he was Chief of Air Force Operations. I thought I better hide it."

Karen peered over. There was a deep hole in the floor, beneath the tile, and from the hole the President had removed a white one-foot-square metal box.

"Give me that," she said, exasperated. She wrenched it from his crabbed hands. "Oh, yes," came more blabber, "we knew the Walker spies were selling our sub frequencies. Army INSCOM people found the mail drop. It was in Odenton, Maryland."

You dick. "Come on." She guided him back to the TV room, sat his ass down. "It was a phone pole they'd mark with white tape," he continued with his tale. "Our men would take the Walker material and switch it with disinformation and fake codes."

"Shut up," she said. She sat with the box in her lap. Red letters warned: RESTRICTED, DO NOT REMOVE UNDER PENALTIES IN ACCORDANCE WITH THE INTERNAL SECURITY ACT OF 1950, USC 790. Her eyes narrowed in curiosity when she opened the box and withdrew an old, yellowed document:

T-O-P S-E-C-R-E-T

HEADQUARTERS, ARMY AIR FORCES
WASHINGTON

06 JULY 47

SUBJECT: Issuance of Classified Orders

TO: Commanding General
Air Material Command
Wright Field, Ohio

1. Notification of confidential orders to be received by the following USAAC and cleared civilian personnel:

> Lt. General Ryan Harding, 0-12366, AC
> Major General Geoff Cooper, 0-14963, AC
> F.B.I. Director J. Edgar Hoover
> F.B.I. SAC Paul Mausbach

2. All above personnel will report to Air Material Command, Foreign Technology Division, in compliance with Emergency Orders via AR-200-1.

3. These orders will be assumed by all personnel as expeditiously as possible.

RE: Confidential material to be transported to AMC, FTD, via USAAC 1st Air Transport Unit, from 509th Bomb Group, Roswell Field, New Mexico.

BY COMMAND OF THE PRESIDENT OF THE UNITED STATES

FM:
DAVID BARNETT
Lt. Colonel, Air Corps
Executive Military Dispatch
Office of AC/FS-1
THE WHITE HOUSE

Hmm, she thought. The TV rambled on: "...the incontestable fact remains, with all the countless thousands of abduction and eyewitness reports, not one single shred of evidence exists to verify the existence of extraterrestrial visitations to our planet. If these things were really happening, someone, somewhere would've produced genuine proof by now."

She picked up another document.

TOP SECRET
SPECIAL ACCESS REQUIRED/EYES ONLY
TEKNA/BYMAN/UMBRA/SI

DEPARTMENT OF THE AIR FORCE
WASHINGTON DC 20330-100

OFFICE OF THE SECRETARY

25 May 1974
SAF/AAIQ
1610 Air Force Pentagon

TO: THE COMMANDER AND CHIEF

SUBJECT: CLASSIFIED REQUEST PER MEMO-
RANDUM (GAO Code 701034); AFR 12-50 (CLASSI-
FIED) Volume II, Disposition of Air Force Records and
Material

(a) Identify pertinent directive concerning crashes of air
vehicles not of terrestrial origin, investigations, wreckage/
debris/dead bodies - retention, recovery, and evaluation.

Dear Mr. President:

Per your request relative to the above memorandum, i.e., the incident concerning the Low Frequency Radar Array (LFRA) detection on 18 April 1974 and disposition thereof. The most notable debris and, of particular sensitivity, all anatomical and post-autopsied remains, have been properly redepositioned amongst selected sites within protected districts of the Army, Air Force, Navy, and Federal Reservations, via recent amendments to AFR-200-1, and so ordered by the MJ-12 Directorate.

> Attachment (TO): -MILNET
> -U.S. Air Force Joint Recovery Command
> -NSA (Interagency Liaison Office)

> Signed,
> Timothy M. McGinnis, Major General O-7
> Commander, Air Force Aerial Intelligence Group
> Fort Belvior, Virginia, MJ-12/Detachment 4

Karen's eyes felt pried open by hooks. *This can't possibly be for.. for.. for... Real.*

"And so ends another edition of *Extraterrestrial Border Line*. Until next time…keep watching the sky."

Next was not a document but a strange wedge of heather-gray material. Thin as newsprint yet sturdy as sheet metal. It wouldn't even bend when she pressed against its corners, nor could she scratch it with the President's boy scout knife. When she held the flame of her cigarette lighter to it, it didn't warp, melt or even blacken, and it didn't conduct any heat. A yellowed sticker, barely readable, stated: PROPERTY OF U.S. ARMY AIR CORP, AIR MATERIAL COMMAND, C/O WATSON LABORATORIES, RED BANK, NEW JERSEY. Another sticker read: EVIDENCE: CORONA, NEW, MEXICO, 198NE, 224S, 5 JULY 47.

Holy...shit...

A song, now, in the background: "With pizza on a bagel, you can have pizza every time!" She snatched the remote. "Turn that shit off, you asshole!" she said to the President.

"Mr. Gorbachev?" he replied. *"Bring down this wall!"* He blew some spittle bubbles as if in contemplation. "Oh, my. I-I think I've got poop in my pants."

Karen may have been able to make a similar claim when she looked back in the box.

≪≪ — ≫≫

"Point Six, this is Team Leader!" Garand shouted into his walkie-talkie. "Report!"

"Team Leader, this is Point Six. We're clear."

"Team Leader, this is Point Four. Clear."

"Team Leader, this is Point Five. Clear. He ain't in the friggin' house."

Garand's mind raged as he fumbled to jack back the slide of his P-226 9mm pistol. The elopement alarm blared like an air raid siren. "Point One, you better get me a fly line to Edwards on the priority band. We're gonna need a tac team out here, and a couple of choppers."

"Roger, Team Leader."

There it all went, like smoke right before his eyes. *My whole life! Twenty years in executive protection and*

I'm gonna go down in history as the guy who lost President Raymond. With my luck, the old fucker probably got picked up hitchhiking out on Route 40 and he's halfway to L.A. by now. He'll be walking into the Hard Rock Cafe telling everyone about the Aurora spy plane, and how we broke Syria's star-net cipher codes and never bothered to tell the Israelis!

Another thought just then, a strangely reassuring one.

Maybe I oughta just put this roscoe to my head right now and drop the hammer...

But before any such consideration could become more transitive, his radio barked. "Team Leader, this is Rover Point. We've got him. He looks okay."

Thank you, God. Thank you thank you thank you...

"Oh, man! You're not gonna believe this! He shit his pants! You should see this, Cap! President Raymond's standing here shaking shit out of his pant leg!"

"Maintain proper radio acumen, goddamn it," Garand said.

"He's got a hard-on too! I shit you not! Stickin' right out his fly!"

"Put a lid on it!" Garand demanded, but he had to admit the image was a doozie: the former two-term president sporting a boner while simultaneously shaking excrement from his slacks. "What's your loke?"

"Past the west lawn. Talk about close. He was hitch-hiking along Route 40."

Thank you, God, thank you! "Bring him in. Is Lavender with you?"

"No sir," the radio replied.

What? That ditzy head queen—where could she be? "Well look around," Garand ordered. "She's got to be out there somewhere."

"No sir," the radio repeated. "No sign of her any-where."

«« — »»

"My name is Karen Lavender of the United States Secret Service," the woman said. Billings glared up. *Another kook but...not a bad looker.* Nice figure under the businessy dress, nice hair, nice legs. *Wouldn't mind pumping one in her,* he mused. *Slick up her slot.* "Look lady, I'm in makeup right now, we're taping in five min-utes and I'm on a tight shooting schedule. You wanna be on the show, fine. Go talk to the line producer."

The woman looked flushed, dizzy, out of breath by some weird kind of excitement she was trying hard to suppress. Her eyes shone hard, steely. Very serious. "I don't want to talk to the line producer, I'm talking to you."

Huffy bitch, ain't she? "Yeah?" Billings challenged. *Maybe she needs to have her ass plumbed. Bet that's what she* really *wants. The good ole spunk enema...*

"Yeah. I'm here to collect the million dollars you're offering for incontrovertible proof of the existence of extraterrestrial life."

Then, onto Billings' makeup table, she set down a big white metal box about the size of a portable televi-sion. *Looks like one of those military courier cases, and very official looking markings.* Then he checked out the documents, and the best piece of "debris" he'd yet seen. *Fuck, this is damn good work.* But still, in this day and age? Forgery had been honed to a state of the art.

"Look, lady, there's hackers out there who can make documents with their PageMaker that look better than this. And this piece of crash debris? *You* may think it's part of a UFO, but I can tell you, it ain't nothing but treated titanium. Believe me, I've seen it all before a million times. Where'd you get this stuff anyway?"

"I stole it from the private residence of former-President Rowland Raymond."

Billings chuckled. *She's good.* "Uh-huh, and I just rode the Merry Go Round with Hillary and Bill. Bill asked me for a hand job."

"There's one more thing in the box," she said. "Take it out. Look at it."

Yeah, she's a huffy bitch, all right. Sort of reminded him of his wife. Only difference was he had no desire to see his *wife's* tits. He'd seen those busted bags too many times. But *this* bitch?

He'd wring milk out of 'em.

Billings peered in the box. She was correct. An acrid redolence, like formaldehyde maybe, seemed to eddy from the open lid.

When he reached in, it was a heavy-duty clear plastic bag that he removed. A sizeable parcel, with some heft to it.

Billings' guts sunk. All thoughts of sex with this woman sunk just as quickly.

Something slack and fat drooped at the bottom of the bag. Kind of a mottled gray color, like slug skin — about a foot long. Billings didn't have to be told that the thing in the bag was a severed alien penis.

THE
ROOM

"But I don't know what to do. Everyone's against me. Even the *press* is turning on me now."

"Don't worry about that," the Senior Advisor assured. "If you let yourself be diverted by that, you'll lose favor with the populace. Your Gallups will plummet."

"So what do I do?"

"Your job. Your job is to lead the country and the American people. They don't care about anything else. Assume the power of your office."

"All right, I hear you. But what about Iraq?"

"You can't bomb them now," the Senior Advisor said. "It's too late. The first time was fine, and that was a fine display of U.S. fortitude. But it's different now."

"Why?"

The Senior Advisor rolled his glassy eyes. "If you bomb them now, you'll have to go for broke. Look what happened to Bush. He waged a *war* against them...but he didn't invade Bagdad. If *you* bomb them now, and you *don't* invade Bagdad and establish a democratic government, then you'll be in the same trick bag only ten times worse. You'll lose your polls for not doing the job right, and then the sex stuff will bury you."

"Okay, then I'll bomb the holy ever living *shit* out of them! I'll send 500,000 troops into Bagdad!"

"Don't be a moron," the Senior Advisor asserted. "If you do that, then you'll have a war with Russia. Hussein owes Russia billions in material loans. If you destroy the Ba'ath Party now, you destroy Iraq's ability to make their payments, which the Russian economy depends on."

"So—so—fuck! What do I do?"

The Senior Advisor nodded with confidence. "You can work it all out under the table…a cool-down period, but just wait until *after* Yeltsin fires his cabinet. Manipulate our aid packages for long-term margins. Ten years from now they won't care what Hussein owes them. You'll be out of office by then." Did the Advisor smile? "Besides— who knows? Who knows what the future holds for Iraq?"

"But…how do you know Yeltsin will fire his cabinet?"

"I know a lot of things. That's why I'm the Senior Advisor," the Senior Advisor said. "True wisdom never dies."

«« — »»

JANUARY 20, 1993

"True wisdom never dies," were the first words he had heard about it—"he" being one William Washington Hilton, the newly-elected President of the

United States, and the words, spoken by an odd little lieutenant general—Reginalds—seemed to eek about the Oval Office like a noisy finch. General Reginalds stood all of five-four, and even with the bald pate and stooped posture, seemed too young to carry the weighty triple stars on his shoulders—early thirties at most—but then the President wasn't about to hold youth against anyone, given that he himself had been elected governor at the same age. Instead, it was the general's creepy, etchy voice that disturbed President Hilton, and the way his tight little hole for a mouth seemed to twitch about the words like the old Clutch Cargo cartoons.

"It even says so in the Bible, Mr. President. 'Wisdom is a light that never goeth out.'"

Hilton leaned back in his chair—the *President's* chair. The chair creaked, like Reginalds' voice. "I appreciate the Holy Scriptures very much, General, but..." Hilton tapped a finger on the leather border of his blotter, a finger that had, not two nights before, been buried to the knuckle in an anonymous vagina at the Omni Hotel on P Street. At the same time, his penis had been buried to the balls in an anonymous mouth...but that was another story. "What I mean, General, is what the fuck does this have to do with me?"

Later that day, the President would find out.

«« — »»

This was little more than twenty-four hours after the President's proper inauguration, and already he'd learned some interesting truths. He learned that Dwight D. Eishenhower and Allan Dulles had authorized the use of atomic weapons against the Viet Mihn in 1954. The devices, in 280mm artillery projectiles, had actually been transported to the field—by the CIA—not fifteen miles from the French fortress of Dienbienphu. But Eisenhower had balked at the last minute when the Soviets suddenly put all of their long-range bomber groups into the air. Hilton learned that subcontractors for the Defense Appropriations and Research Programs Agency had been experimenting with microwaves and radiation on unsuspecting civilians and military personnel for the last forty years, and that these experiments were still going on. He learned that the CIA had indeed used reconnaissance and intelligence aircraft to transport heroin during the Vietnam War, and that they now did the same to transport cocaine from Mexico and South America—all for ten-percent net to be used for operations that the U.S. Congress would not approve. This all sounded fine to Hilton. All for the greater good. Hell, why shouldn't the United States grab some of that profit? Dimly, though, he wondered how much of that same cocaine had gone up his own nose in days gone by.

"You have many modes of advisement at your disposal, Mr. President." Now Reginalds was leading the President down the West Wing, past the Cabinet Room and the press offices. Hilton spied a pretty blond intern and gave her a wink. *Fuck it, I'm the Prez now. I don't have to worry about my own state troopers squealing on me.* He'd have to tell Bruce to arrange a little executive meeting tonight. *Maybe Blondie could use a raise, and I'll give her one—the Big Five-Inch raise. And goddamn Jen for telling Penthouse that I've got a small dick.* The President didn't care. *It works and it spits. You don't need a big dick when you're the most powerful man on fucking earth.*

"Mr. President?"

Reginalds was looking at him as though slighted, as though there was some reason this geek Army general required Hilton's undivided attention. "What?" Hilton snapped.

"I was commenting that as the chief executive you have many modes—"

"I heard you, shorty. Many modes of advisement at my disposal."

"Correct, Mr. President. You have Central Intelligence, the Joint Chiefs, the Cabinet, the NSC, every senatorial and congressional committee."

"I graduated from Yale. Don't you think I know that, dickhead?" the President asked rather testily. Then he paused, appraising Reginalds' squinty frown. "Yeah, that's right," he said. "I just called you a dickhead. And you wanna know why?" Hilton cut a grin.

"Why, Mr. President?"

"Because I can." Then the President cracked out a laugh that boomed down the ornate hallway.

"Really, Mr. President. We have important business."

"Look," Hilton countered. "I don't even know who you are, except that maybe you're the *shortest* mother-fuckin' general in the history of the U.S. Army." Hilton jabbed his thumb into his own chest. "All I know is this: I'm the fuckin' President of the United States, and I've got *shit* to do. *Important* shit. I've got health care to nationalize and the deficit and a big fat defense budget I gotta slash. So what happens on my first official day as President? I get a call from the Chairman of the Joint Chiefs of Staff and I get another call from the *former* Secretary of State, and they're both telling me the first thing I have to do is have a conference with *you*. Well, here I am, shorty, and this better be good 'cos if it ain't, you're gonna be the shortest *private* in the history of the U.S. Army."

"Follow me, please, Mr. President."

Hilton was just getting used to it. *Mr. President.* He could dig it; it had a nice ring. He followed Reginalds farther down the plushly carpeted hall, when they passed the White House Travel Office. *Yeah, we'll be getting those assholes out of there faster than shit through a goose. Get our regular folks in there like we had down home, keep those kickbacks a-comin'!* "Would you at least tell me where we're going, half-pint?"

"We're going to the The Room, Mr. President."

Hilton craned his neck like a pigeon. "The Room? You mean, like, the *bathroom?* Shit, how about if we just say to hell with it and I piss on your leg?"

"That's your prerogative, Mr. President," Reginalds stonily replied, "if you so desire. But I have my orders, and my orders are to take you to The Room. After that...feel free to urinate on my leg."

The President rubbed his crotch. "I feel a long beer-pull comin' on, shorty. So let's get on with it."

The last quarter of the West Wing was restricted. Reginalds showed his ID to the Marine at the door, and then the Marine robotically nodded and punched in the keycode. A door with bolts like a bank vault chunked open. "Try making *me* show an ID, jarhead," the President said, "and I'll have you shoveling seal shit in fuckin' Alaska."

Reginalds led him on. The corridor stood dark, pin-drop silent. For some reason, the tiny hairs on the back of the President's neck stood up. "What is this place?" he asked.

"Just an ancillary sector, Mr. President."

"Ancillary sector? Are you trying to insult my intelligence?" The Chief Executive, in truth, didn't know what the word ancillary meant, in spite of three degrees. "I'd like to kick your ass. How do you like those beans, huh? And you wouldn't be able to do a thing."

"No, Mr. President, I wouldn't. Part of my Army induction oath, the oath I took when I was commissioned, and my Tekna-Dinar-grade National Secrecy Oath, all required an unwavering vow of loyalty to the President of the United States."

"So you'd do anything I said?" the President egged on.

"Yes, Mr. President."

"So if I pulled out my cock and told you to suck it, you would?"

"Yes, Mr. President."

"You'd smoke my pole like there was no tomorrow and swallow the nut, and then say 'Thank you, Mr. President. May I have another?'"

Reginald's shoulders slumped and he very traceably sighed. "Uh, yes, Mr. President."

"Okay, chrome-dome. On your knees." Hilton brought his hands to his crotch, grabbed his zipper tab. "Let's party."

Reginald sighed again, and began to lower himself to his knees.

President Hilton cracked his hands together and laughed. "I'm just kidding, applehead! But I'll bet I had ya goin' there for a minute, right?"

Poker-faced, Reginalds answered, "Yes. Sir. As a matter of fact, you did."

Hilton chortled on, walking. "Well, that's one thing you and your Secret Service boys don't have to worry about. It's chicks only for me. I ain't no homo."

Reginalds nearly smiled at the remark. He'd seen these guys come, and he'd seen them go, but Hilton was by far the worst, even worse than Reagan. But the fact remained, the F.B.I. and the Army's Defense Investigations Service had incontestably uncovered at least three homosexual events in the President's past, once in college while attending Georgetown University, at a fraternity kegger after an anti-war rally, and twice at the governor's mansion in 1982. He'd been horny as all get-out after tooting some of that Super Coke his brother had brought over, so they'd just said to hell with it and performed fellatio on each other. The President-to-be had even swallowed; what a trooper! Reginalds, however, elected not to mention these tidbits to Hilton. It could be used as a trump card down the road, and the little general had a funny feeling he'd need it. *Better that this pompous ass NOT know that I know...*

"So. Where did you say we're going?" the President asked.

"The Room," Reginalds replied.

《《 — 》》

Another door with bolts like a bank vault chunked open. "What is this?" the President complained. "Some fuckin' bomb shelter or something?" but that's all he said for the moment. When he looked at the clerk sitting at the sign-in desk, Hilton simultaneously pissed and shat his trousers.

Sitting at the sign-in desk was—

"Is that-is that-is that," Hilton jabbered, the front of his pants wet, the back full and warm.

"Yes, Mr. President. It is," Reginalds answered.

"But-but-but," Hilton continued to jabber. Now he was shaking fairly firm stool out of his Armani pant leg. The feces flapped to the floor. "It-it-it… It CAN'T BE!"

"Things aren't as they seem, Mr. President. You will learn many things in The Room, things that you would have, until now, believed to be impossible." Reginalds cleared his throat. "And, yes, sir. It *can*, indeed, *be*."

The man sitting at the sign-in desk, distinguished, bald with white hair on the sides, tall, gaunt, pencil moustache, and somehow still debonaire in his excessive if not impossible age, was a famous actor named Vincent Price.

"Think of it as a reallocation of technology, Mr. President. Extending the life of paramount minds and utilizing them as resources. For our betterment. For the greater good."

Hilton's eyes bugged; he was flabbergasted…as an unpleasant smell rose. "Technology?" he blurted. "Resources? What the fuck are you talking about?"

"Specify your query, and I'd be happy to accentuate, Mr. President."

The President pointed maniacally, hopping on one foot as he shook more stool out of the other pant leg. "The guy in *House of Wax* is sitting at the desk, alive! He died in the early 90's!"

"Indeed he did, sir," Reginalds answered. "We call it biological refurbishment. We restored him, with *technology* recovered in the wreckage of a crashed extraterrestrial vehicle."

The President's eyes bugged further, like a caricature. "You mean a-a-a—"

"A UFO, for all intents, sir."

The wet spot on the front of the President's slacks

grew to an odd shape. "Roswell," Hilton whispered. "All that stuff on the *X-Files*...is true."

"Roswell, Mr. President, is malarky. Disinformation generated by the U.S. Air Force to divert the attention of the populace away from the *real* extraterrestrial contacts. We've had exactly eleven such contacts since 1947, from which we've culled an enormous amount of technology. Low-light and infra-red optics, hydrogen and kinetic energy propulsion, electro-magnetic-pulse direction. Even microwave ovens. In this instance—in April, 1962—NORAD tracked a UFO skimming across North America at divergent speeds and altitudes. It crashed near Nellis Air Force Base, in Nevada. The crew was rescued by a second vehicle but despite the damage, the vehicle itself remained reasonably intact. CIA and Air Force Technical Services retrieved quite a bit of very interesting technology. One such technology was the aforementioned, Mr. President: the ability to regenerate the dead."

Hilton shot alternate glances from Reginalds, to Price, back and forth, back and forth. "So you...regenerated...Vincent Price?"

Reginalds shrugged. "The President at the time was a big fan of *House of Wax* and *The Conqueror Worm*. Call it an eccentricity. And don't worry. Mr. Price isn't anything close to what you might think of as a zombie. He's quite coherent and very effective at his job."

The esteemed star of *House of Wax* rose, tall, graceful, statuesque. He looked just as good as he had in his last movie, *Arabian Knight*. He smiled humbly, offered a hand to Hilton. "It's an honor to meet you, Mr. President," he said in that world famous voice. "I've always been a staunch supporter of your party."

"Thuh-thuh-thank you," Hilton replied to the "refurbished" gentleman.

"And I assure you, I'm quite sound of mind and very qualified for these duties. I'm not just an actor, you know. I studied at Yale, at several venerated schools in Vienna, the Courtald Institute, and the Academy of Nurnburg. How do you like that?" The former actor smiled again, a classic. "I'm more educated than you are."

Hilton gaped.

"This way, Mr. President," Reginalds urged.

Hilton walked uncomfortably, most of the poop in his pants evacuated, but not all. From behind the anteroom branched a series of hallways; Hilton followed the tiny general into what seemed a central corridor, which was darker than the others yet so immaculate it shined. The only sound to be heard were their snapping footfalls. Eventually, Hilton's voice overcame his incredulity: "Who else has been...rejuvenated?"

"Not many. It's quite a costly procedure. But there are several, all of whom you are familiar with in one way or another. Nixon, Lodge, Humphrey—quite a statesman by the way, even though he lost. Oh, and we've also got former house-majority leader Tip O'Neill—"

"I love that guy!" Hilton celebrated.

"—former Central Intelligence Director William Casey—"

"I hate that shifty ghoul!" Hilton railed, face reddening.

"—and a few others, most of whom have been installed as presidential advisors of the first water."

This is serious business, Hilton realized. *The most important men in the country...are dead!*

The corridor ended in a nice, well-appointed waiting room; Hilton thought of a dentist's office. Quiet. Innocuous paintings on the wall. Dark, subtle tones and a soft burgundy shag carpet that silenced their footfalls on the corridor's previous linoleum. Hilton's nose skrinched at the wafting odor of his feces when he eyed the waiting room's obvious distraction.

Ah-OOOO-gah! he thought with a flare at his groin.

A woman sat on the low couch, like a hybrid between a runway model and the ultimate brick-shit-house beach bunny. Long tan legs crossed out from a tight denim skirt—a very very *short* skirt—and a diaphanous black-silk blouse that made no secret of 36D state-of-the-art implants. Platinum-blond hair shimmered at her shoulders.

"Who's that kick-out-jambs piece of box?" Hilton whispered to the general.

"Think of her as a sub-contractor, Mr. President. There's quite a bit of activity back here—however discreet."

What did that mean? "Take some advise, shorty. Stop jerking me around or I'll have that Marine out there box your fuckin' ears. Give me a straight answer. Who's the brick shit-house? She looks like something out of a Victoria's Secret catalogue."

"Actually, sir, she was their cover girl for two years, until we…appropriated her."

"Appropriated?"

"We pay her well, to serve her country in a unique manner."

Hilton was infuriated. He walked up to the girl. *What's her problem?* he wondered with some irritation. *The President of the fucking United States of America is walking up to her and she looks like she's about to fall asleep.* "Hey, honey. I'm Will Hilton. Who are you?"

A petite snore was his response.

The bitch fell asleep! He nudged her. "Hey? Honey? This is my house. Who the hell are you?"

Droopy eyes fluttered open. "Huh?"

"Who are you?!"

"Stacy," she mumbled.

"Well what are you doing here?"

She sighed, exhausted. "I'm waiting for Snowdrop."

"Who the hell is Snowdrop?!"

Stacy winced at the volume of the question. "She's my friend. We come here every week. We're regulars."

Hilton raised a serious brow. *Regulars? This sounds very fishy.* "Look, this is my fucking house, *Stacy,* and I have a right to know what the fuck you're doing here. Why are you sleeping on my couch?"

Annoyed, she turned, pouting. "I'm worn out! I'm tired! Leave me alone!"

"Leave you alone? Don't you know who I am? I'm the President!"

"Oh," she said. She fell back to sleep.

"Start talking," Hilton ordered Reginalds and looked at his watch. "You've got ten seconds before I call in that big jarhead and order him to pop your eyeball out and stuff it up your butt so you can see him kicking your ass."

Reginalds sighed wearily. "The women who come here are sexual therapists, Mr. President or—in terms you can better relate to—prostitutes. We hire them to sexually placate all of our biologically refurbished advisors."

"Now you're talkin', shorty." Hilton jacked his pants down, shitty undies and all, and walked up to Stacy. He extracted his flaccid penis (which, verifying popular belief, did indeed sport and ungainly mole on the glans) and nudged the woman awake. "Hey!" he blared. "Wake your ditzy ass up and meet the Executive Balony Pony!"

The girl squirmed awake with a whine. "Leave me al—" When one eye fluttered open, though, her complaint changed in tenor. She squinted. "That looks like a penis...only smaller."

Hilton shuddered but before he could go into a conniption, another door clicked open, in a little cove beyond the waiting room couch.

Hilton stared, incredulous.

A petite sound grew closer: "Ooo, ooo, ooo," and with each "ooo" he noticed a silhouette taking an awkward step. The utterance, too, was clearly female.

Who is THIS splittail, I wonder? Hilton thought, peering into the cove's shadow.

Eventually a completely naked woman emerged from the cove. She was limping, uttering "Ooo, ooo, ooo" with each step, as if in pain. From her fingers dangled a pair of Bally high-heels and draped over her forearm was a pretty vermillion dress. She was every bit as attractive as Stacy, and then some, with stunning shining perfectly straight red hair, peaches and cream skin, and—

That's the best fucking set of tits I've ever seen in my fucking life, Hilton observed, mouth gaping.

Big pink nipples budding from the frost-white orbs of flesh made the President think bon-bons on balls of white chocolate.

"Ooo, ooo, ooo," the woman limped on, then— "Ahhhhhhhhhhhh," when she flopped naked on the couch next to Stacy.

"Who are you?!" Hilton demanded.

The redhead looked up critically. "Snowdrop. And who are yoooooou?" she asked with instant distaste.

Hilton glared. "I'm the fuckin' President!"

"President of what?"

The President ignored the ridiculous question. Surely, she was joking. Instead, his mind was diverted. *Shorty said these girls were hookers, and I can't think of a better time for them to start hooking.* "Hey, Snowdrop?" he addressed. "How about a little—"

"Yuck, you stink like a load of full diapers," she interrupted. "Could you not stand so close to me?"

Jesus!

"Stacy," she whispered to her friend. "It just keeps getting better and better."

"I know. Can you believe it? And we're actually getting *paid* for this."

Snowdrop sighed blissfully. "I've...just...never met a man...like him... I've never come so hard in my *life*."

Hilton listened with some disturbing interest. It was obvious: the man they were talking about wasn't him. "Never met a man like who?" he demanded.

The girls both giggled, huddling together on the couch.

Hilton stomped over to Reginalds, the last of his patience burning up. "What the hell's going on here? I'm not getting anything out of these bimbo skillet-heads. So *you* tell me, and if you keep pulling my chain I'm gonna turn you into the fuckin' White House Toilet Boy. I'm mean, I'm the President, for dick's sake, and they could shit care less about me. When I was governor I couldn't walk down the goddamn street without ten chicks begging to smoke my pole. Who's this other guy they're talking about?"

Reginalds frowned. "Who he is, sir, isn't nearly as pertinent as what he can do for you."

"I don't want *him* to suck my dick, ass-head; I want those bitches on the couch to do it!"

"Forget about the girls for now, Mr. President. You're facing a crucial dilemma in—"

"WHO'S THE GUY?" Hilton bellowed.

Reginalds frowned as presidential spittle dotted his face. "The guy, Mr. President, is right behind that door..."

The general was pointing.

Hilton followed the direction into a recess off the wall. It was dark. A door faced him, clearly the door the two call-girls had just exited, and on it hung a brass plaque that read: SENIOR ADVISOR.

Hand trembling, the President opened the door. His eyes bloomed when he peeked in. But before he could enter fully, an almost cliched Massachusetts accent shot forth:

"Goddamn it. Would somebody bring me my chowdah!"

THE
HICCUP

They knew that he hated the Soviets, and it was the Soviet GRU operative who'd fronted the initial money for the job. LeBelle, however, understood the technicalities more than Peroni. It was true, Peroni was the shooter, LeBelle the spotter. But LeBelle was the brains of the mission. He was in the Marseille Mob with all those connections, plus an active freelancer for SDECE. He had all that experience in Algeria; he'd even come close to killing DeGaulle in 1960. "Missed by an inch," he'd regretted. He'd used a modified M2 caliber-fifty and Unertl 3.5x scope. "An inch, and we'd have been done with the traitor of the Fifth Republic." At any rate, Peroni had every confidence in the man and, besides, he preferred to be told what do to.

"So who are these GRU guys?" he asked, uncapping the scope. "Like KGB, right?"

"Worse," LeBelle said in his clipped action. He prepped the ammunition: 50-grain .221, the highest velocity pistol ammunition ever produced by a major manufacturer. They traveled at 2640 feet per second and, however small, would take a man's head off at 100 meters. "They make your CIA look like boy scouts, and they know that the target hates the Soviet Union. He must be eliminated. That simple."

"So why are my people involved too? And yours?" Peroni asked. "There's a lot of folks in this mix."

"We have much easier access in and out of the country, thanks to Giancana's delegates in Brownsville. That's why we're doing the job instead of them. The U.S. INS and CIC screen well for Russians and Mafia. But not us."

"Why?"

LeBelle chuckled. His colleague really didn't know much, did he? But that was all for the best. "Kennedy's father has been in bed with the Mob—your people—since the 20's. Bootlegging, mostly."

"Oh."

"They also know that Kennedy can't win the next election—not with the Catholic issue, the infidelity with the German woman which is about to be raised in the Senate, and not with the problems in Southeast Asia."

"Oh, yeah," Peroni seemed to recognize something. "That Vietnam place."

"Yes."

More GRU operatives, in collusion with scouters in the Marcello-Trafficante crime family, had picked the perfect sniper's nest. The second-floor of the Dal-Tex building. A perfect firing-lane, and since Marcello's people had already set up the fall guy, everyone would think the shots had originated from the book depository just ahead of them, across from the records building.

It was clockwork.

The scope, also a Unertl, had already been calibrated and zeroed. And the weapon?

Peroni held it up as a father might raise a newborn. "It's beautiful, ain't it?"

"Yes. It is."

The XP-100, just released by the Remington company, shorter than a rifle, longer than a pistol; in fact, that's what the XP stood for: "experimental pistol." The ultimate close-range sniper weapon.

"So what's my range again?" Peroni asked.

"Approximately 80 yards."

Peroni chuckled. "Frenchy? I can pick *cherries* at 80 yards."

LeBelle didn't doubt it. He'd coached Peroni at Trafficante's camp in Florida. This would be the biggest "cherry" of his life.

The next 15 minutes ticked by like hours. It always happened that way. The streets were packed but quiet; the scene down below seemed nearly tranquil. But when the cheers began to flow, they knew it was time.

"Assume your firing position," LeBelle said.

Peroni sighted, the window opened about ten inches. The Secret Service wouldn't worry about an opened window this far back from Elm Street. LeBelle sighted too, with a Zeiss monocular. In its bright field, he could see the motorcade turning the corner, followed by the long black Lincoln convertibles.

"Wait, wait…"

"I know," Peroni calmly complained. "I can't get a front shot—those fuckin' trees."

"Wait, wait for them to pass, fire from behind, just as we practiced in Florida."

In his ears now, LeBelle heard nothing of the crowd. Silence. Until—

"Take your target," he whispered.

Then, two sounds occurred almost simultaneously.

One: "*HICK-up!*"

Two: BAM!

The weapon barely bucked. Peroni keeled over, the XP-100 clattering to the floor. He brought his hands to his face. "Holy shit, man! I hiccupped when I squeezed the trigger! Tell me I didn't do what I think I just did!"

LeBelle didn't move. He couldn't. He kept his eye in the monocular, watched the chaos as the motorcade sped away, no doubt, for Parkland Hospital. *My God,* he thought.

"Tell me!" Peroni pleaded. "Tell me!"

LeBelle, now, lowered his monocular. "Your target was the second car, not the first."

"I *knoooooooooooooooooow!*"

"The Soviets realize that Kennedy can't win the next election. He would lose the nomination to Johnson, and Johnson would win because of his harder line against communism."

"Who was that guy I just shot?!"

"Johnson was the contract target," LeBelle said in a voice like crumbling rocks. "The man you just killed was Kennedy himself..."

HAUNTED HOUSE

"That ASS-mother-fucking-HOLE!" bellowed the President of the United States, and Josh W. Burnet had been exactly that for a little less than twenty-four hours when he'd made this first official executive profanation. Veins bulged at his forehead. Three Secret Service men looked back at him, speechless. Burnet had tempered himself against the first several mishaps...but *this* was too much. The Presidential Inauguration yesterday had been a big bust: freezing rain. Protesters had made Burnet and the Vice-President arrive last to all seven inaugural balls, and then the presidential limo had broken down. Hence, the executive protection staff had had to drive Burnet and his lovely wife Lenore to the White House in a Toyota Camry that belonged to a reporter for the *Washington Times*. And when Burnet had been given the reason for the limo breaking down, he'd been told with some reluctance that it was a clogged fuel filter. Someone had put sugar in the gas tank.

"That's an outrage!" Burnet had loudly replied to the news. "That's deliberate sabotage!"

Indeed. It couldn't be proven, of course, but Burnet knew that the slimy shyster—one Wallace Jackson Canton—who'd moved *out* of the White House yesterday was behind it all. Popping all the W's out of every computer keyboard in the West Wing was just for starters. 8x10 glossies of split beavers in the xerox machines, skidmarks on the Presidential towels, more split beavers loaded as screensavers on the Presidential monitors. A few cheap shots on the way out the door; Burnet shouldn't have been all that surprised.

Calm down, calm down. The President pinched the bridge of his nose, then re-addressed his SS men. "I apologize, guys. My gosh—the president, using such awful language. Don't, uh, don't tell the press you heard me cussing, huh?"

"Of course, Mr. President," one of them said. "We'll be right outside if you need anything. The Chief of Staff will be in shortly. Until then, why don't you relax?"

The President smacked his hands together. "That's a great idea, son! I think I will."

The detachment left the Oval Office. Just after the door clicked shut, Burnet realized the wonderful gravity of his situation. Finally, after all that work and all that campaigning... *I'm...the President.* God had been with him. Burnet saw this as providential: he was the light of truth for the New Millennium. The people had said so on election day. Burnet was now not only the leader of their government but the symbol of their hope. After an eight-year hootennany of illegal fund-raising, infidelity, and $10,000 haircuts, it was time to get the country's respect back.

And I'm the man for the job, Burnet thought proudly.

A hot frown lit his face when he noticed today's edition of *The Washington Post* set out for him on the Presidential Desk, and it wasn't the headlines that caused the frown (DOW PLUMMETS THIRD DAY STRAIGHT, ACLU CRIES FLORIDA VOTE-COUNT "RIGGED," and WILD ANIMAL ATTACK KILLS SIX IN SOUTHEAST D.C.); instead it was the paper itself. Burnet dropped it in the Presidential Wastebasket. *From now on, it's The Times. No motherfucking way The Washington Post will ever be in MY White House. Liberal ass-kissers. Bet they never kiss MY ass.*

He shoved the aggravation off. He wasn't going to let these little things ruin his day, his *first* day as the chief executive for the most important county on earth.

No. No motherfucking way. Not the liberal press and its sniping, not the most offensive and dishonest newspaper in the western world, and not even his predecessor's deliberate pranks. This was the greatest day of Burnet's life, and he was damn fucking well going to enjoy it.

"I think it's time for me to take my first sit-down in the most powerful chair in America," he told himself. He pulled the grand chair out and sat right down.

squish

Burnet's expression froze. *What the hell?* Then something warm and mushy spread out over his buttocks.

And the odor rose.

Burnet jumped up, glared down at the cushioned seat of the Presidential Chair, and then shouted so hard and loud his chest ached: "That goddamn cocksucking ass-motherfucking-HOLE!"

Someone had left a fresh human bowel movement for him to sit in.

«« — »»

Burnet was antsy that night. Actually he was horny, but Lenore wasn't much into sex these days—hormonal changes, she'd said. *Shit,* Burnet thought to his hard-on. Being the most powerful man on the surface of the earth would have to be enough. No motherfucking way he'd wind up pulling stunts like his predecessor. *I'm the beacon of the world now,* he reminded himself. He was in this proud 130-room house by God's divine choice. Yes, it had to be God. Even the spiritual world had its cycles and its checks and balances. *We just had eight years of self-serving, Godless evil,* he thought, *and now the tables have turned. A servant of God is back in the White House. Me.*

He'd gotten up, cloaked in his Presidential Robe. He liked the fit. Up here on the second-floor stretched the Presidential Residence. Burnet looked down the hall which eventually led to the south-lawn portico—the hall stood quiet and dark, though he knew a veritable shit-load of Secret Service stood on post just down the stairs. They'd highly recommended that several SS men maintain watch up here, but President Burnet had expeditiously said "Fuck, no" to that. He didn't want to hear a bunch of goons walking back and forth while he was trying to sleep.

He stood there now, in the open bedroom doorway. He was looking out into the dark hall. "At least we won't have to listen to lamps being thrown against the wall anymore," he heard an SS man say from downstairs. "And no more dead bodies in Fort Marcy Park." "Let's hope," another answered. "I just wonder how Joshy-Boy will react when he finds out the whole deal."

Joshy-Boy. So that was his nickname? *That's me they're talking about,* Burnet realized. He padded quickly to the stairwell, to listen. *The whole deal?*

"They usually take it rough at first. Reagan was a real pain in the ass, and Carter didn't even believe it until the hostage thing. Word is that's what sealed the deal."

What the fuck are they talking about? Burnet thought.

"I'd do it. Shit. To be president?"

"Me, too."

"Canton hasn't had the talk with him yet, has he?"

"I don't think so. If he had, Joshy wouldn't still be stomping around here like a redneck Napoleon."

Heat began to waft off Burnet's face.

"Probably tomorrow would be my guess. They never wait too long. Canton doesn't want to hang around D.C. is what I heard. Gonna move to Harlem."

"Harlem?"

"Yeah. Wants to be white Superfly."

Chuckling. But Burnet was duped. *Canton hasn't had the talk with him yet...* The talk? *The FUCK is that?*

Then a better question occurred to him. *Why don't I just ask those hammerheads? I'm the fucking president.*

Burnet was about to tramp right down the stairs and demand an explanation, but...

A cold gust of air tickled his neck. A draft? *There better not be, not in the fuckin' White House!* He turned around immediately.

And stared.

A paunchy bald man stood at the end of the hall — correction: a pudgy, bald *naked* man. Burnet couldn't make out the face — it was too dark. *There's a naked fat guy standing in the hall,* came the stark thought. *In the White House.* Burnet dared himself to approach the figure but the necessary courage didn't quite surface.

Then the figure began to approach *him.*

Burnet yelled for the SS men from the top of his lungs…but no sound came out. Zilch. And the pudgy bald guy advanced but as he did so, his feet didn't move. He was *drifting* toward President Burnet. Pale as wax, hollow-eyed, belly sticking out.

That's when Burnet recognized the man: the 36th president of the United States, Lyndon Baines Johnson.

This is fucked up!

Johnson's voice seemed to flutter, like winged insects. His lips barely moved. "Where's the barbeque?" From beneath his paunch, he extracted his penis, flaccid but formidably large. He flapped it around. "Take a look at that bad boy, huh?"

"But-but-but," Burnet stammered. "You're dead. You died in 1973."

"Yeah, but I passed the Medicare Bill, didn't I? And I kept General Dynamics in business. When I got elected to my first term as senator, I had 800 dead people vote for me. Did you know that?"

Johnson's lifeless whisper seemed to be everywhere. "I'm lost," he drawled next. Fuckin' Khrushchev, that little fat commie dumpling. We bitch-slapped him, didn't we?"

I must be dreaming, Burnet felt assured. *LBJ is NOT standing here holding his dick in front of me.*

Johnson flapped the penis again, like raw flank steak. "Where's Madilyn? I need to squeeze the guts out of this snake, knock her up again. Which way to the ranch?"

The figure urinated liberally onto Burnet's leg. The

piss smelled like whiskey and beef barbeque. Burnet couldn't move.

"Have fun in the new house." The figure was drifting away, feet not moving. "Don't trust Putin—he fucked animals when he was a kid."

LBJ floated down the hall, then disappeared into a door. He didn't open the door and simply enter. He *dissolved* into the door.

Yeah, nightmare, Burnet thought, keeping his composure. He bit his hand and almost yelled. *All right, it's NOT a nightmare, so it must be—*

A ghost.

Sure. Why not? It's long been said that the White House was haunted. Lincoln, Rutherford B. Hayes, and Eleanor Roosevelt's lesbian lover (what a bag!) were frequently spotted prowling these halls at night. Burnet could live with it.

But then he wiped his fingers against his leg; they came away wet...and smelled like piss laced with whiskey and beef barbeque.

Do ghosts piss?

The door that LBJ has disappeared into read NO ADMITTANCE, PRIVATE ARCHIVES. Burnet jiggled the knob. Locked. *I'm the fucking President for God's sake!* he railed. *No admittance, my ass!* But where could he get a key? The Secret Service men downstairs? Burnet thought better of it. *What, I'm gonna tell them that the ghost of LBJ wagged his dick at me and pissed on my leg and then he walked through that door?*

Probably not a good idea.

Fresh air, that's the ticket. He scurried back down the hall, went out on the portico which overlooked the south White House lawn. *Better, better!* He was regaining his composure, yes, but this was still pretty fucked up. If it wasn't a dream and it wasn't a ghost, then it must've been a hallucination, and presidents weren't supposed to hallucinate. Not cool.

But I'm not crazy. This is ridiculous!

"Just calm down, just calm down," he said to himself and even chuckled. What a situation! Nothing more than nerves, he decided. A guy goes through almost a year of campaigning—he's entitled to freak out a little. It would pass.

Sure.

He gazed out onto the nighted yard—*his* yard. It was cold, still drizzled freezing rain, and he'd heard that this was officially the worst weather to ever befall a presidential inaugural week. Burnet wasn't discouraged, however. The lousy weather only reminded him that life was full of obstacles—it was supposed to be—and great men welcomed those hurdles. He had many a task ahead of him yet he would tackle each one with vigor and confidence. Black money would fund the B-3 bomber, so that was no biggie. But the school-voucher plan? *Might be tough,* he considered. And with all those milquetoast, panty-wearing bunch of Harvard Yard closet socialist liberals in the Congress—Burnet had to admit—getting that bill to pass would be like parting the fuckin' Red Sea. And then there was his campaign promise, the across-the-board tax-cut, which would be even harder to pass. But—

Be strong. Have faith.

There. Now he felt *a lot* better. Past the grounds, he could see the beautiful Anacostia River, and when he looked to the left, he could see the street he officially lived on: Pennsylvania Avenue. Then he saw—

The FUCK?

There was a man running across the south lawn, right toward the house. And the man—

Holy motherfucking SHIT!

—the man was wearing a turban, a beard, and swishy black robes. A terrorist. *This is the White House! What kind of dipshit security system do we have here!* Burnet opened his mouth, to scream out a warning at the top of his lungs but, lo...

No sound came out. Zilch.

Where was the Secret Service? Where were the guards, the perimeter defenses, etc.? *Some towelhead extremist just jumped the fence and nobody's doing anything about it!*

But a moment later, somebody *did* do something about it. A second figure ran out into the yard. Unmindful of the rain, he seemed to be dressed in a dark double-breasted suit and tie. His face was bone white and so was his hair, and he must've been in his sixties. Yet he ran down the terrorist like a cougar running down a woodchuck. And—

What was he doing now?

That guy's GOT to be too old to be a Secret Service operative, Burnet speculated, but nevertheless, the gray-haired man stopped the terrorist in his shifty tracks, and now he seemed to be...

Burnet blinked.

He'd bitten down hard on the terrorist's throat and was sucking his blood. It didn't take long. The terrorist convulsed in the grass. The gray-haired man sucked and sucked. When he was done, he smacked his blood-smeared lips and grinned up at Burnet on the veranda. The two fangs were more than apparent. He waved a death-white hand at Burnet and then ran off.

I-I-I…I don't believe what I just saw.

More hallucination, more stress. He squeezed his eyes shut and told himself, "There's no vampire on the grounds. Lyndon Johnson is not a ghost haunting the White House, and when I open my eyes there will not be a blood-drained terrorist lying on the lawn."

President Burnet opened his eyes.

There was a blood-drained terrorist lying on the lawn, only now several Secret Service men surrounded him, shining down flashlights as another whacked a wooden stake into the trespasser's heart. Moments later, the body was carried away.

Burnet rubbed his face. *I only had three glasses of champagne at the ball.* Then there was that vodka tonic at dinner, but still… *That's not enough booze to make me see things. Is it?*

Hmmm.

He looked up into the sky as if expecting God to look back down at him and offer encouragement. A moment later the freezing rain abated and the clouds began to part.

There! See? Things are getting better already!

Where the clouds parted, he could see a full moon.

Shit, it's late as a motherfucker, he realized. *I better go back to bed,* but when he turned around—

Whoa!

Back inside, at the end of the hall near the stairwell, he saw another figure. The figure was squatting: knees jutting out, buttocks split. It wasn't Johnson, either; the figure looked slimmer, and dark.

It was defecating on the carpet .

There's the motherfucker who shit in my chair!

President Burnet was not surprised this time when

he attempted to shout at the top of his lungs but no sound came out. He rushed back in. One way or another, he was going to get to the bottom of this.

The figure stood back up, its business finished. On the carpet lay a glistening, rich caramel-brown bowel movement the size of a birthday cake; its depositor seemed pleased with its size. But by then Burnet had stopped running forward; he stopped as effectively as if he'd run into a brick wall. His eyes seemed lidless as he looked back down the hall.

The figure was covered head to foot with matted hair, its face vulpine. It grinned naughtily, extended a taloned hand and gave Burnet the finger.

A werewolf.

Yes. A *werewolf* just gave the President of the United States the finger…after taking a giant shit on the floor.

The werewolf was gone when Burnet looked again, but the pile of excrement was still there.

"Josh! What are you doing out there? Come back to bed, Tiger."

Tiger? His wife, Lenore—that is, the First Lady— had spoken the words. She was standing in the half-opened bedroom door. She'd never called him Tiger before. Additionally, the tone in which she'd called him this sounded rather, uh, lascivious. Lenore *never* sounded lascivious. And she would *never* stand in the opened bedroom doorway completely naked.

Yet completely naked she stood.

"Come back to bed…"

Burnet, even in spite of just witnessing a werewolf defecating on the floor of the White House, was taken seriously aback. *What a fuckin' brick shit-house,* he thought, looking back at her. It had been a while since he'd seen her so brazenly naked. *The old broad's really holding up. Man!* Big large-nippled breasts stood out full and without a trace of sag. Stomach so tight you could bounce a quarter off it, and legs going clear into tomorrow. And another surprise: she'd, uh, mowed the front yard.

Holy motherfucking SHIT!

One hot little hand reached up, grabbed his arm. The other hot little hand reached down, grabbed his genitals through the robe. The Presidential Flagpole was *up*. She began to pull him back into the bedroom.

But something reminded him of what he'd just witnessed in the hall. He pulled back, stuck his head back out the door.

"Come on, Prezzie-wezzie. What are you looking at? What's out in the hall that's more interesting than me?"

He couldn't very well answer *A pile of werewolf shit, honey,* now could he? He surrendered to the evening's strangeness...but not before stealing a final glimpse down the hall.

A Secret Service man was pushing the heap of excrement into a dust pan with a piece of cardboard, while two maids stood by with buckets and brushes, preparing to shampoo the rug.

Lenore dragged Burnet back into the bedroom and closed the door. She hauled off his robe; before he could even get on the high four-poster bed slept in by every president since FDR, Lenore got to work. She kept him standing up, got on her knees behind him, and—

Wooo!

The very last thing President Burnet would have

ever expected was the very naughty sexual act known as analingus but—

Woo-woo!

—that's what he got just for starters, and starters was about all he could manage just then. When she simultaneously reached around and gave the Presidential Joint a soft, single stroke, Burnet's face screwed up like Shemp's and he launched the Presidential Jizz all over the bed.

Aw, jeez! He was looking forward to his first Presidential Lay, but there it went all over the sheets in just a few seconds.

"Don't worry, Tiger," her hot whisper drifted up to his ears. "That was just the primer. We're gonna fuck all night…"

"My oh my," Burnet replied. The prospect sounded peachy to him.

Indeed, she fucked him all night and then some. Burnet hadn't had this much sex in one night since college. But the room was dark and—to be honest, certain preternatural monkeyshines were taking place, and said monkeyshines were the reason Burnet never noticed that Lenore was sound asleep on the other side of the bed during the entirety of the escapade.

But if his wife was sound asleep on the other side of the bed, who was this woman who looked just like her, riding him like a donkey?

«« — »»

Next day, President Burnet met with the House, the Senate, and the Joint Chiefs. Each time after he spoke, the great halls of Washington, D.C., thundered with applause.

Burnet could dig it. Later, he met with the Director of Central Intelligence and the Chairman of the National Security Council. Everything went smooth as a baby's backside. Throughout each meeting, though, something nagged at the back of the President's conscience. *Should I tell any of these guys that last night I saw a vampire on the south lawn? Should I mention that the ghost of LBJ pissed on my leg, and a werewolf took a shit on the floor? I guess I better not.* Burnet still didn't know what to make of all that but if he indeed had been hallucinating, it probably wouldn't be prudent to make this information known. He didn't want to go down in history as the first chief executive to be relieved of his office due to psychiatric problems. *It was all probably just a dream,* he told himself, even though he knew that couldn't be the case. And as for the mongo sex with Lenore last night? She'd acted quite strange this morning. "You were great last night, honey," he'd told her upon waking, with a big fat kiss. "Huh?" she'd replied, and fell back to sleep. Burnet wondered if their hours-long coupling had really happened…but if it hadn't, what were all those stains on the sheets? A whole lot of *something* had been spilled, and Burnet didn't think it was Kool-Aid.

He worked the new Presidential Chef's ass off for dinner, inviting most of the Cabinet and their wives, plus a few senior senators. (But not Ted Kennedy. *Fuck him,* Burnet thought. *Somebody oughta drive* HIM *off a bridge.)* Whenever Burnet had made a humorous remark at the table, everyone had laughed uproariously. Burnet dug it. Later, just before bed, the President had gone back into the kitchen to personally compliment the chef but the kitchen was clean and empty. He really wanted to scarf a few more of those wasabi-and-creamed-salmon appetizer puffs. *Where do they keep leftovers in the White House?* he wondered. He was about to go ask the Secret Service guys out front but—

What was that noise?

Sounds like someone eating.

Burnet, in Presidential Robe and Slippers, followed the sound. After turning a few corners, he found himself entering a sizeable pantry lined on one side by commercial refrigerators. And—

Who the fuck!

One of the refrigerators stood open, and in front of it stood an absolutely obese man with a busy mustache. He was munching on something from the refrigerator.

"Who the hell are you?" the President demanded, rushing up.

The man was huge and...he stunk.

Burnet's rush forward halted as abruptly as if he'd had a door slammed in his face. *Jesus!* The stink was so bad, he almost gagged, and now that he was a few feet closer, he got a more detailed look at the interloper in the light coming out of the refrigerator.

Fuck...

It was a 400-plus-pound corpse standing there, in a shredded long-tailed jacket and corroded slacks.

"Good evening," came a garbled introduction. "And congratulations on your electoral victory." The words sounded like someone talking and gargling at the same time, and even through the visage of green rot, Burnet recognized the man:

William Howard Taft, the 27th president of the United States.

"You're a-you're a—" Burnet began but couldn't possibly finish.

"A zombie, yes," Teddy Roosevelt's secretary of war replied. "It seemed an ideal choice." From a silver platter in the fridge, Taft was picking off the dainty salmon puffs and popping them into his maggot-lined mouth. "Or I should say, an ideal choice for me personally. Zombies eat."

They sure did. By the looks of it, Taft had not only decimated the leftover salmon puffs but had wiped out damn near everything else in the refrigerator.

"Zombies don't really eat dead flesh or human brains," the former U.S. Solicitor General added. "That's just a cliche. But ghouls—now *they* eat dead flesh and human brains." Taft popped another puff into his jowly mouth. "These are quite good, by the way. You should have some."

"I'm not going eat those things after a motherfuckin' *zombie's* had his fingers on them!" Burnet understandably yelled. But then he thought: *Well, at least he's a Republican and a Yale man.* "What are you doing in the White House?"

"It's part of the deal."

"What deal?"

"It is well-known fact that presidents are called upon to make crucial decisions. You'll find out just *how* crucial presently."

"What are you talking about!" Burnet screamed.

More munching. "I was buried in a piano crate. Did you know that? And here's something else you probably don't know. I'm the only president to later be appointed Chief Justice of the Supreme Court."

This is crazy, Burnet thought. *I really am cracking up.*

"Good luck with your tax cut…"

Taft was walking away, his zombie belly sloshing like a beer keg. *Zombies, werewolves, vampires, ghosts...* What could he do?

I just won't tell anyone, he convinced himself, walking back toward the stairs. *So what? I'm a little nuts. Lincoln was a little nuts but he did a fine job running the country. They say James K. Polk was a bit of a nut-job too, but he got us the Panama Canal and passed the Walker Tariff Act.*

Yes. But did they see monsters prowling around the White House?

Burnet didn't want to consider that question.

Newscaster words drifted toward him. "—the Washington, D.C., police spokesman said shortly after the witness died at Georgetown Hospital. Other sources told CNN—"

Burnet frowned sharply. The Secret Service man at the desk before the stairs was watching a small television.

"What the hell are you doing watching CNN, son? I gave specific orders yesterday that CNN will *never* be watched in the White House. Ted Fuckin' Turner. Bunch of liberal pimps!"

The man jumped up. "Very sorry, Mr. President."

"Change that channel to Fox Network News right now unless you want your ass sitting guard at our embassy in fuckin' Chad this time tomorrow."

"Right away, Mr. President," the spit-and-polish sentinel replied. But just before he switched the channel, Burnet could've sworn he heard the CNN newscaster say: "—some kind of wolf."

Did he say wolf?

"—offered no comment when asked about witness reports of a 'wolf-like' animal leaving the scene near the

Adam's-Morgan area of Washington, D.C.," the Fox-News correspondent was saying after the channel had been changed.

"Did he, uh, did he say something about a..." But Burnet let the question fade.

"What's that, Mr. President?"

"Nothing."

Burnet straggled up the stairs. *A wolf?* He'd read something in the paper too, hadn't he? Yesterday? Something about a wolf...

He needed something to get his mind off all of this, and when he climbed into bed he got that something. Lenore lay sleeping next to him. Burnet popped the fastest erection of his life when he recalled their smorgasbord of sex the night before. *Yeah,* he thought. *I need some more of that...* But when he nudged her and pleaded, "Honey? Wakie-wakie. Prezzie-Wezzie needs some action really baddie-waddie," she flinched away and mumbled, "Go jerk off!"

The President felt stung. *Do I gotta win a national election every time I want to get laid?* What a disappointment...

"Hostile bitch," he griped under his breath. Her suggestion, however, left him with little choice, but he wasn't comfortable doing it in the bed right next to her. Even the President had some pride. He retreated to the Presidential Bathroom, which was bigger than, say, most mid-list novelists' entire apartments, and sat down on the Presidential Toilet Seat, and after briefly wondering if it really cost $600, he got down to business. He grabbed the Captain and began to jerk.

His head felt flushed with leftover images from last night: Lenore's naughty tongue roving his balls, Lenore's succulent breasts in his face, Lenore's hot legs spread apart like a wishbone about to snap. *Jesus,* he thought, eyes squeezed shut and pumping. *This ain't gonna take long…*

Burnet's butt flexed on the padded seat, but right before he would ejaculate, a voice interrupted, "Crankin' off a quick one, huh?"

Burnet fell off the toilet, shouting, dick still in hand. Someone was in the bathroom with him! He crawled backwards into the corner, desperately yanking his robe closed. His eyes bugged out toward the shower.

A man was standing there, and not just any man, either. It was his arch-enemy and predecessor, Ex-President Wallace Jackson Canton.

"You!" Burnet howled. "I sent you packing yes-terday! This is *my* house now! What are you doing here?"

"Watching a president beat his meat." Canton stepped out of the shower, wearing casual jeans and a flannel shirt. "But I gotta tell ya, Joshie, it's tough jerking off when you're president. They've got these damn pinhole surveillance cameras everywhere."

"GET THE FUCK OUT OF—" Burnet blinked. "Whuh… Did you say…*cameras?*"

"Damn straight. Those SS fuckers are everywhere — it's their job. Canton pointed to a speck on the wall. "See? There's one." He waved at it.

Burnet felt on the verge of a stroke. "You mean they just—"

"Saw you chokin' the chicken? I'm afraid so. But don't worry about it. In the White House? They've seen a lot worse than that."

Burnet jumped up, tried to compose himself. This was crazy!

"And you've got more important things to be

thinking about." Canton lit a cigar, then offered one to Burnet. "It's a Cuban, a Monte-Cristo. Try one."

Burnet quailed. The end of the cigar looked darkened, as if dipped in something. "Get that thing away from me! And what are you doing here? I thought you were moving to fuckin' Harlem!"

"Oh, I'll be dropping in every once in a while—we all do. It's part of the privilege." Canton toked the cigar. "I understand you've seen a few of us already."

The President stared at the comment. Canton's face seemed to shift through the smoke. "Since you succeeded me, it's my job to fill you in on the whole schmear. You know. The rest of the deal."

The deal. Burnet felt woozy. Hadn't Taft said something similar? *It's part of the deal,* the corpulent zombie had told him.

"Does this have something to do with the ghost of LBJ pissing on my leg?"

Canton smiled. "Not really a ghost. A subcarnate. I'll bet the piss smelled like beef barbeque, didn't it?"

"Oh, and Taft!" Burnet added. "He's a zombie! I just saw him in the kitchen, and last night...I saw a vampire out on the south lawn!"

"That could've been any number of ex-presidents. Pierce, Filmore, Harding—oh, and Jefferson. Jefferson's a vampire. Vampire is a popular choice."

"And-and-and...and a *werewolf!*" Burnet shouted, spittle flying. "I saw a *werewolf,* in front of the *stairwell!* And he took a *shit!* Right there on the floor!"

Through the cigar smoke, Canton floated Burnet a snide grin. "That was me."

The President went limp in place. "You're telling me you're a werewolf? *That's* what you're telling me?"

"Yep. There's a—how do I phrase this? Think of the deal as a contract, a legal and binding memorandum of agreement between two parties. One paragraph of that contract has an option provision. That's why I'm a werewolf now, and that why Taft's a zombie, and that dim Texas fuck Johnson is a subcarnate. You get to choose, and I chose werewolf. And, yes, I'm the one who took a shit on the floor last night, and in your chair." Canton tossed a casual shoulder, savoring the cigar. "It's an impulse, I suppose. Like marking territory? Werewolves are very territorial. I took a shit in here too." Now Canton's hand bid the shower stall, and come to think of it, Burnet smelled something, didn't he?

He peeked in. "Holy moly!"

The defecation sat firmly stooled on the shower floor, neatly coiled around and rising to a peak. It must've weighed five pounds.

"That's a lot of shit!"

Another toss of the shoulder. "Werewolves eat a lot. Haven't you been reading the papers? Sudden rash of savage murders in the Capitol Hill area?"

"That was *you?* You killed those innocent people?"

Canton's grin sharpened. "No one is innocent."

"This is bullshit," Burnet concluded after another moment. "I can't believe I was taking you seriously for a minute."

Canton abruptly pointed down. "Shoe's untied."

Burnet glanced down, then frowned. He wasn't even wearing shoes, he was wearing slippers.

"Fooled ya," Canton said.

Burnet shouted when he looked back up at the former president. What stood in front of him now was full-fledged werewolf, pointed ears, canine snout, claws, fur and all. "Believe me now?"

Just more hallucination, Burnet reasoned.

"And don't try telling yourself you're seeing things. The only thing you're seeing is a *werewolf* who used to be president. I'm one of the eternally damned now. I sold my soul to the Devil; in exchange, the Devil gave me everything I wanted while I was in office. Within reason, of course. How do you think I fixed up Bosnia? How do you think I kept the House happy when Newt was Majority Leader? Hmm? Why do you think the *Senate,* a political body that hated my guts, voted not to proceed with impeachment hearings?"

"The-the Devil?"

"Satan protects the powerful. And what is a president? The most powerful man on earth. Anything you want—within reason, of course—you'll get. *If* you join the team."

Burnet suddenly felt exhausted. He sat back down on the toilet, rubbing his face. "You mean—"

The werewolf continued puffing the cigar. "I mean unless you want your name to be mud in the history books, unless you want your administration to fail miserably, you have to agree. You have to invite the Prince of Lies into your heart, give your soul to him and vow to serve him. Do that, then all your dreams come true."

A werewolf is telling me I have to sell my soul to the Devil, Burnet recited to himself. *Why does fucked up shit always happen to me?*

"It's easy, and it's not really that big a deal. Now that you're President, what do you want more than anything?"

Burnet chuckled dryly. "I want the *House* and the

Senate to pass my tax-package, but there ain't no way that's gonna happen. Not in a million years."

"Wrong. Agree to the deal and it *will* happen. And lots of other great shit too. Anything you want."

Burnet looked up from his pathetic seat. "Yeah? Well what if I *don't* agree to the deal?"

"That would be a big, big mistake, my friend."

Burnet was actually chuckling now. "I'm supposed to believe that every single man to ever be sworn into this office sold his soul to the fuckin' Devil?"

"Not *every single* one," the transformed Canton explained. "There were a few suckers who said no, or changed their minds in the middle of the deal. If you want to be the most powerful man in the world, you've got to compromise a little. You've got to get with the program. JFK didn't, and look what happened to him. Went right behind the Man's back and initiated the Alliance for Progress and the Peace Corps. Some balls, huh, and it all happened right after Satan bailed him out of the Cuban Missile Crisis. Kennedy didn't get with the program, and neither did Garfield, Lincoln, or McKinley and look what happened to them. Why do you think Zachary Taylor died after only being in office for sixteen months? He said no to the deal. And William Henry Harrison? Tippecanoe, my ass. That Whig moron was cold a month after his inauguration. Satan offered him the deal and he said no. And look at FDR. Satan gives him *four terms* as president and you know what the ungrateful son of a bitch tries to do? He tries to close down the Manhattan Project! Well, Harry Truman took care of that problem lickety-split. What's the moral of the story here, Joshie? Join the team…or die."

"I'm not selling my soul to Satan for shit's sake," Burnet sputtered.

"Then you're fucked, buddy-boy. You'll never get that tax-cut passed. But, shit, you won't even be in office long enough to bring it before the House."

"What are you talking about!" Burnet argued with the werewolf. "I'm doing that next week!"

"Your VP will have taken over by then." Canton produced a manila folder. "Once these pictures get sent to the right people, your ass is grass."

"What pictures!"

Canton removed a stack of 8x10 glossies from the folder, passed them to Burnet.

Burnet gasped.

The pictures showed a very naked President Burnet in bed with a very naked and very young girl.

Very young.

Every conceivable sexual position was demonstrated in the photos, and some not so conceivable.

"Whole lotta shakin' goin' on last night, huh, *Prezzie-Wezzie?*" Canton sniped.

More spittle few off Burnet's lips when he objected, "I had sex with my *wife* last night, not this-this-this—"

"Child?" Canton finished.

"Her name's Jezzinine, Lilith's daughter," Canton explained, "and one of the Four Whores of Gomorrah. She's a *haggurath*, Josh, a shape-shifting succubus. She can make herself look like anyone: your wife, a ten-year-old little girl, Pam Anderson, or your mom, for that matter." Canton cast an approving glance at the top photo in Burnet's hand. "In truth, she's several thousand years old, but in that picture, she looks like a fourth-grader, huh? And that's really all that matters, wouldn't you say? Her appearance to others?"

Burnet glared at the werewolf with choked-up rage.

"You tricked me! You made me think this monster was my wife! You're blackmailing me!"

"Something like that. Call this an inducement. Ooo, what do you think the Republican National Committee would say if they got a gander at these? What would the *public* say if they saw these in the *National Enquirer?*"

"This is outrageous!"

"Oh, don't let this influence your decision. You don't *have* to agree to the deal. That would actually be very commendable, sticking to your true morals and all that." Canton pointed down to the pile of werewolf shit in the shower stall. "Oh, you better clean that up. You wouldn't want your wife to see it, would you?" Canton laughed. "She'd think *you* did it. She'd think her husband—the President of the United States—took a giant dump in the shower!" Canton took his fur-covered body and wild animal musk toward the door. "I've got to go chow down on some Washingtonians, but I'll stop by again one night next week." He passed Burnet a key. "And take a peek in the archives room right down the hall. Some pretty cool stuff in there, might help you get the picture."

"I'm not going—not going to do it!" Burnet shouted. "I'm not going to sell my soul!"

Canton grinned through fangs. "You'll sell it. Satan's got a big agenda this year, Josh, and we've all gotta pull for him. Join us, Josh—" He pointed to the pictures in Burnet's hand. "—or next time it'll a *boy's* butt you're using for a party. A *little* boy's butt."

《《 — 》》

The next few days passed without mishap. Er, well, without global or national mishap. In the White House, there were *all kinds* of mishaps. Large piles of animal excrement were found in unlikely places—Burnet himself had inadvertently stepped in a few of those piles—but they were discreetly cleaned up by the Secret Service and housekeeping staff without a word. Someone kept eating leftover hors d'oeuvres out of the refrigerator every night, leaving an atrocious death-stench, and Burnet's dog—a loving, energetic cocker spaniel named Skippy—was found dead in the South Wing. The White House vet had stutteringly explained that the dog had died from a common canine liver disorder called hepatic thrombosis, but it sure looked to Burnet like somebody had drained all of the mutt's blood. It looked like a friggin' bag of hair lying there! "What are those two holes?" the President asked, but the stammering vet assured him: "Uh-uh-er, Mr. President, oh *those* holes? They're uh-uh-uh—biopsy perforations. That's it! I needed to perform a biopsy. Those holes are from *biopsy* needles, Mr. President." "On its fuckin' *neck?*" But Burnet let it pass. Several more vicious incidents were reported in the Capitol Hill region, people savagely mauled, mutilated, killed. An animal attack, the papers claimed.

When Burnet awoke on the morning of his sixth day in office, Lenore angrily shoved him awake:

"Josh, what have you done! My God!"

"Whuh-what?" Burnet groggily leaned up.

He felt...wet.

"You *wet the bed!*"

She escaped to the bathroom, disgusted. When Burnet sat up, he found himself drenched, the covers sopped. *Did I really piss the bed?* he wondered, but then he realized that the bed's pervading dampness smelled an awful lot like whiskey and beef barbeque. Then:

"FUCK!" he shouted when he picked up that morning's newspaper sitting outside the bedroom door on its silver platter. Not only was it the *Washington Post,* the headlines read: INSIDERS SAY HOUSE MAY PASS PATIENTS' BILL OF RIGHTS AND TRADE PROMOTION PACKAGE, BUT "NO WAY" TO TAX CUT.

"FUCK!"

Consciously, he forced himself to ignore his little meeting with the werewolf several nights ago. Subconsciously, though, his mind was ticking away. His campaign promise had been the tax-cut; if he didn't get it, he'd be lambasted by the press and populace alike. Subconsciously, too, he canceled that day's luncheon with the Senate Finance Committee. When asked why, he replied, "'Cos I fuckin' feel like it! Blow me! Those old fuckers aren't gonna pass my bill anyway, so fuck 'em! Tell 'em to have lunch at fuckin' Burger King!"

Next thing he knew, he was unlocking the door to the White House Archive Library on the second floor of the residential wing.

Where did I get this key? he asked himself but when he summoned the answer, he blocked it out. *Canton. A werewolf! It was all just a nightmare...*

squish.

He didn't even look down to see what he stepped in. The stuffy library extended before him. He half-expected ghosts to greet him but there were just books, racks of documents, and file cabinets.

Where am I supposed to look?

A drawer by a barred window slid open, squeaking. It opened by itself. Burnet sat down and found a stack of photos looking up at him from the drawer.

Oh, man...

First photo: Richard Nixon, as a ghoul, digging up corpses in Arlington Cemetery.

Second photo: Lyndon Johnson, a naked subcarnate, urinating into a punch bowl during a last year's Presidential Christmas Gala. No one could see him, yet his image was clear on the photo.

Third photo: three werewolves, Grover Cleveland, Franklin Pierce, and Ike Eisenhower, were playing croquet out on the south lawn. They looked like they were having a blast.

Fourth, fifth, and sixth photos: tuxedo-garbed vampires getting out of elaborate coffins: Woodrow Wilson, Calvin Coolidge, and Gerald Ford. Ford, evidently, had stumbled while getting out of his, and fell to the floor.

There were more photos, too, verifying what Burnet had already been told. Many more presidents had clearly made the same deal, and had elected to spend eternity as some manner of monster. These pictures were proof.

And some of them had been damn fine presidents! Men who'd gone down in history, with greatness. (Well, not Coolidge.) *Is this really what I've got to do?* the President wondered, shuffling out of the library. *For my country?*

He gritted his teeth.

No!

Damn it! There was no way in Hell Burnet was going to sell his soul to the Devil just to get what he wanted as President!

"Help me! Help me!" a tiny voice peeped. Burnet looked aside. A little girl, grade-school age, had accidentally wandered past the cordons which read: WHITE HOUSE TOUR PATRONS, PLEASE DO NOT STRAY PAST CORDONS. Then Burnet's eyes bolted open. A slim man in a gray pin-strip suit had the little girl in a corner, his mouth clamped to her throat. The little girl quivered as her blood was drained.

"Stop that!" Burnet yelled.

Jimmy Carter looked up, licking glossy red lips. The girl was a withered husk now; he let her crumple to the floor. "That's a damn sight better than peanuts," he drawled. "Her parents were registered Republicans."

"Get out of here, you hick vampire!"

Carter straightened his tie. "You're going to join us, right?"

"No!"

"Don't be a dumbass." Fangs glinted through that big famous southern smile. "Join us." He began to slink away.

"Hey!" Burnet shouted after him. "Did you kill my dog?"

"That was Harding. He's a creep."

Carter was gone. Now a bat was fluttering away.

«« — »»

"Join us…"

Burnet was drowning, eyes squeezed against the hot gush. And there was that damn smell again! Burnet loved Texas barbeque but…not like this. He sat up, drenched, frowning, and as he did so, he saw the corpulent and liver-spotted LBJ—always naked—fading away.

"Don't be a cracker. Join us."

Burnet sighed when the apparition was gone. Why didn't the urine disappear too? He just shook his head. Lenore's side of the bed was empty; she'd taken to sleeping in another bedroom. Burnet couldn't blame her, considering the nature of the wake-up call. His face dripped urine when he got up. *Is that liberal cocksucker gonna piss on me EVERY MOTHERFUCKING MORNING?*

But he couldn't help but consider: maybe it would stop if he...

Joined them.

The door opened and the morning manservant—a skinny Japanese kid in black slacks and a white wasitcoat—rolled in Burnet's standard breakfast: Eggs Benedict and cheese grits. The kid didn't say a word about the obvious fact that the President of the United States was sopped from pajamas to skin with urine.

"The eggs better be medium hard," Burnet warned.

"Ah-so, Mr. Pwesident."

Burnet lifted the silver platter lid, and gawped. There were bitemarks in the eggs and several fingergrooves through the grits. "You gotta be shitting me!" he railed. "Someone's been eating on this!"

"Sir?"

"Don't *sir* me, you skinny punk!" Burnet stared at him. "Christ, you look like Fuji on *McHale's Navy!* Take this shit out of here and bring me my breakfast!"

The kid bowed several times, reeling the cart back out of the room. Before the door reclosed, Burnet spied William Howard Taft smiling back at him, chewing.

That zombie tub of shit! Hadn't he eaten enough in life?

When Burnet was in the shower, he sensed ghost-faces looking at him. Were they looking at his groin? Smiling? One of the faces looked just like Harry S. Truman. Burnet winced through the rest of his shower, winced again when he got out to dry himself and noticed the words JOIN US, SHORTY written into the steam on the mirror. A literally ghoulish Richard Nixon was rummaging through Burnet's underwear drawer when he came out.

"Leave me alone!"

Nixon loped away, carrying the stench of fresh-dug graves with him. There was dirt all over Burnet's underwear now. *I can't believe I voted for that son of a bitch...*

When the Japanese manservant reappeared with the breakfast cart, Burnet said, "If there are any bites out of this, I'm shipping your ass back to Nagasak—"

But the man had already left, practically running out of the room.

Burnet lifted up the platter lid. His face screwed up at once, at the heavy odor. This time the pile of feces was actually steaming.

Burnet threw the lid against the wall with a clang, then fell to his knees, his fists clenched, and he shouted, "All right, goddamn it! I'll do it!" and the words echoed up and down the impeccable halls of the White House like a cannon going off.

《《 — 》》

Canton was virtually chugging another cigar as he sat with his hair-covered feet propped up on the Oval Office Desk.

"We knew you would. Anyone with degrees from Harvard *and* Yale can't be that stupid."

Burnet sat in a chair opposite, nearly choking in the smoke. "And no more leaving piles of shit around, right?"

"I promise. You're one of the team now."

Burnet rubbed his hands over his face, sputtering. "I can't believe I'm about to sell my soul for eight years of success as president."

Canton, ears pricked, leaned up at the comment. "Or maybe just four."

Burnet jerked his gaze. "You got eight years, you motherfucker! I want eight too. For Christ sake, I won't lose a re-election! I'll be the incumbent! Who's gonna beat me! Gore?"

Canton shrugged one shoulder. "Four years, eight years, what difference does it make? You'll still be a successful president."

"You *know* something!" Burnet felt sure. "The next election's already rigged—by the Devil!"

"Just don't worry about it," Canton dismissed. "They'll be the best four years you could ever imagine. Come on, Josh, be real. How else are you going to get that tax-cut passed?"

All right, all right, just remember it's for the good of the people, Burnet reminded himself. "I guess I also have to decide what I want to be…after my term is up, huh?"

"Oh, you mean your eternal curse. Right. Werewolf, vampire, ghoul, zombie, subcarnate—anything you want. You can even be a cacodaemon. That's a demon that eats Satan's shit."

"I don't think so!" Burnet hollered.

"Or you can be an incubus." Canton winked. "Really lay some pipe with the ladies. Pick the one that suits you best. But you don't have to choose right now. You choose on your last day of office. For now, don't worry about it. Just get ready for all your dreams to come true. You're the most powerful man in the world. It's a trip, man."

Burnet looked astonished as Canton got out of the chair and made to leave the room. "What, that's it? Don't I have to sign a contract or something, in blood?"

Canton smiled, showing black-pink wolf gums. "You just signed the contract, Josh. With your heart. Toodles!"

Canton hulked out of the room, leaving Burnet flummoxed.

«« — »»

The very next day the House and the Senate unanimously passed Burnet's Omnibus National Tax-Cut Package. Burnet was hailed the people's hero. The Zogby and Gallup Polls measured the President's approval rating at ninety-six percent, the highest in history. And that was only the beginning...

FOUR YEARS LATER

"Close the door, grapehead," the President ordered the Secret Service man. The door clicked shut, and the President looked around the grandiose Oval Office. *All mine*, he thought, *and it's about fuckin' time. I'm gonna have a BLAST as President. I'm gonna ROCK!*

He stroked his beard, appraised his face in the reflection off the highly polished desk top. *First since Garfield, I think. Chicks'll dig it.*

"Hey! Get back in here!"

The Secret Service man re-entered. "Sir?"

"Who was the last President to wear a beard? Was it Garfield?"

"Yes, Mr. President."

"Well, what about Chester A. Arthur?"

"He had muttonchops, sir, not a full beard."

"I thought so. Thanks. Now get out."

The Secret Service man raised a finger. "Just a reminder, Mr. President, but the first inaugural ball begins in a half hour. You'll have to start getting ready."

"I'll get ready when I damn well please, dick-for-brains! I'm the President. Now get out!"

The door clicked shut again. *God, I love yelling at those guys.*

It would be a grand night indeed. All those parties? All those women oogling him? *Fuck yeah. I'm a chick-magnet now.* It had been kind of a weird day, though. Burnet had been grinning through the entire swearing in. The new President couldn't help but notice that; in fact, he'd almost flubbed a few lines of the Oath of Office. *What's that cock-sucker got to smile about? I just kicked his incumbent ass out of office. I pulled sixty-percent of the vote.*

Same thing during the ceremonial Last Ride. Burnet had been in the back seat of the limo with him, on its way to 1600 Pennsylvania Avenue. They'd smiled at each other and shook hands for the cameras. But then Burnet said the strangest thing, as he was about to get out of the Presidential Limousine for the last time.

"See you in a few days," Burnet had said.

"I won't be seeing you ever again, ass-rag," the President replied. "*I'm* the Big Cheese now, *I'm* the Daddy-Mack. And what are you? Old news."

"How are you gonna get that National Health Care Package passed?"

The President was outraged by the brazen question. "That's my business! Now get out of the car. Or I should say, get out of *my* car."

"Like I said, see you in a few days," Burnet told him. "We have to talk."

The President laughed at this absurdity. "We have nothing to talk about ever again. You lost. So let's make these my official last words to you: Tongue my balls, Mr. *Ex*-President."

Burnet held that weird grin of his, then he winked...and closed the car door.

That guy's nuttier than a Pay Day...

No, the new President had big plans: bust the previous administration's tax schedules, cut defense, get back the Death Tax, oh, and save the whales. Not to mention the legislation that would forever carve his name in American history—National Health-Care coverage. Plus he had a lot of chicks to impress, with the new beard!

But the moron at the door was right. It was time for the first Inaugural Ball. *Better get ready...* He began to head for the door but something caused him to pause. Was there something he should do first?

"Ah, of course..."

He was President, after all! It was high time he took his first seat in the most coveted chair in the world, the *Presidential* Chair.

He walked back to the desk, pulled the chair out, and sat down.

squish

www.ingramcontent.com/pod-product-compliance
Lightning Source LLC
Chambersburg PA
CBHW070706280626
47159CB00022B/2248